Pat

Enjoy The Wo..

THE UNIMAGINABLE WEALTH IN THE EYE OF THE MOON

THE UNFATHOMABLE SERIES OF ADVENTURES
BOOK 2

By Tim and Kathy Hunt

TKHunt Books
Copyright 2021 ©

ISBN: 9798508568795

THE UNIMAGINABLE WEALTH IN THE EYE OF THE MOON

TABLE OF CONTENTS

Chapter 1	Page 11	Chapter 8	Page 123
Chapter 2	Page 27	Chapter 9	Page 139
Chapter 3	Page 43	Chapter 10	Page 155
Chapter 4	Page 59	Chapter 11	Page 171
Chapter 5	Page 75	Chapter 12	Page 187
Chapter 6	Page 91	Chapter 13	Page 203
Chapter 7	Page 107	Chapter 14	Page 219

Chapter 15   Page 235

Chapter 1

The Unimaginable Wealth In the Eye of the Moon

He stood six foot, three inches tall and wore a black longcoat given to him by Lord Bennington. The rest of his outfit made one think of a British explorer save his hat which would seem to belong on a newsboy in New York rather than the man who had saved the world countless times. His name; McAlister Chance.

I am quite obviously not six feet tall and nowhere near his physique. I am a bit plump with graying hair and a full beard resembling Father Christmas. I dress in full explorer gear right down to the over-sized pith helmet. My longcoat is buckskin and was given to me by Wild Bill Hickok. I am Dr. Winthrop Corbyn, Archeologist Extraordinaire.

Chance is married to the love of his life, Miss Zadie. She is a linguistics expert and hieroglyphologist and quite good at it, I must say.

I, on the other hand, am not married. I am an explorer and I simply don't have the time nor the inclination for such falderal and balderdash.

It was Miss Zadie who summoned me to their home on this occasion. I arrived precisely on time, as usual. I was met at the door by Chance himself, "Chance, old friend. What seems to be the urgency?"

"You're late, as usual, Winnie. No matter, Zadie is waiting for you in the study." Chance bellowed with half a grin.

"Late!? Plusterpot! I am never late." I tramped toward the study door, "What are we up to? Has she found a tomb location?"

"Go! She will tell you." Chance hurried me in through the door.

I hadn't but entered the room, when, "Winthrop! You have to see what has been found. Come, quickly." Miss Zadie was standing over the desk.

"What is it?" I hurried over. I looked down at the desk at what appeared to be old tintypes. I looked at the old photographs and saw ancient carvings in stone, "What are these?" I put on my spectacles.

Miss Zadie was giddy as a schoolboy… or rather schoolgirl, "My friend, Charlee, in the States, found these in an old box of thing taken from ancient Anasazi structures."

"Anasazi? Ancient North American people who flourished from around 200 BC to some five hundred years ago?" I had to make sure I was thinking of the same people.

"Exactly and then they just vanished. I've been studying these since they arrived. They are clues left by the Anasazi." She was quite excited.

I was excited now as well, "Clues to what?'

"I'll tell you if you will just let me get a word in." She looked at me over the top of her glasses.

"Yes, of course, forgive me, my dear." I looked back down at the tintypes.

"They are about their great wealth and where it is hidden." Miss Zadie went on, "This one translates basically to 'We had to hide our wealth from the bad people.' Marauders I would suppose."

"Wicker fugglies." I added.

Miss Zadie looked at me, "Wicker fugglies?"

"Yes those that would destroy everything you've worked for." I explained.

Chance smiled at Miss Zadie, "Just carry on."

She looked back at the tintypes, "And this one says, 'Our wealth… of a size not to be understood… is placed or hidden in the eye of the moon.'."

"Of a size not to be understood? What does that mean?" I questioned.

"Well, that's what I don't understand. What this shows is that it is bigger than everything the moon shines on, which would be impossible. I am assuming it is very large." Miss Zadie looked at me over the top of her glasses again, "The large tintype says that only the sun through the heart of the Thunderbird will find its way to the eye of the moon."

I turned and looked at Chance. There was a man standing behind him, "Heavens, who is that?" I stammered reaching for my revolver.

"Easy old friend, Bartholomew (Bartholomew was their butler, never missed a day of work in his life) had a family emergency and the agency sent Marvin here to take his place." Chance explained.

"Would the Madam like s'more tea?" Marvin asked.

"Yes, please." Miss Zadie held out her cup.

Marvin walked over and handed her the tea pot.

At that moment, the front door slammed open and Bartholomew's voice rang out, "Where is that pompous imposter!? I'll push him into the ground like a tack! Tie me up and take my place will you? I think not!"

We all looked back at Marvin. Miss Zadie looked him in the eye, "You're not from the agency, are you?"

He smiled at her, "There ain't no agency, Miss." He reached down and scooped up all of the tintypes and jumped out through the window, sending glass flying everywhere. He rolled to his feet and began to run. Over his shoulder he yelled back, "The professor thanks you."

I walked to the broken window, ripped off my spectacles and watched him running, "Von Duggery!" I growled wanting to pull my revolver, but I knew there were too many innocent people who might get hurt in a firefight.

"You know him?" Miss Zadie asked.

"The Professor? Yes, Morley Von Duggery, a blight upon us all." I said.

"A wicker fuggly?" She attempted to use my word.

I stepped closer to the window to see Marvin, or whatever his name truly was, hand the tintypes to someone in a steamer, "The wickerest fuggly of them all." I watched the steamer drive off with Marvin hanging from the rear, laughing.

"Who is this Professor?" Miss Zadie asked.

Chance and I looked at one another. We had both run across him before, "A thief and a scoundrel. He waits for others to make discoveries and then reports them as his own, before the true discoverer has time to report their findings." I said turning toward her, "He will undoubtedly already be telling the Historical Society what *he* translated off of those old tintypes."

"Yes, and they will believe every word and will undoubtedly fund his expedition. His uncle is the Minister of Antiquities." Chance added.

"Then we should get there first. Charlee knows where these places are… well, maybe not the 'Eye of the Moon', but I am sure it won't be hard to find." Miss Zadie began walking out of the room.

Chance looked at me and then at his wife. "Zadie, dear, where are you off to?"

She stopped and turned back to us, "To pack of course. And you should do the same. There is a dirigible leaving for New York within the hour. I'll have Charlee meet us there." She turned and started to walk, "You won't want to be late for that airship, believe me. I would be quite upset." Her voice echoed through the house and within my brain.

"Chance, what about your son?" I asked.

"He's digging up that old toll road you sent him to, remember? He won't return for months." He smiled, "Now, you should go pack as that lady will not be happy if you are just 'precisely on time'." He laughed at my expense and went off to pack his things.

This whole time, Bartholomew had been standing just outside the study. He had watched the imposter jump out the window and listened to all that was said. He looked at me, "I believe the madam is of earnest, sir."

My eyes opened wide, "For the love of cumquats, I had best pack light. Miss Zadie is quite formidable when she is upset." I darted out the door and straight home.

Jamison, my valet, had me packed and off to the Aero Docks in a matter of moments. I arrived almost three minutes early. I carried both of my bags up the loading dock to find Chance and Miss Zadie waiting for me there, "You're late, as always, old friend." Chance chuckled.

"You truly are an impertinent swine, do you know that? I am three minutes early and have packed extremely light." I sat my bags down in front of me.

The porter came and picked them up, "Nice to see you again, Dr. Corbyn."

I looked him in the eye, "Weldon Muddly! Mudd! So good to see you again. How goes things with Miss Riley?"

"We was married at Christmas and are as 'appy as a couple of bugs in the butter. We owe it all what to you and Mr. Chance here. We most likely would never 'ad said a word to each other without you." Mud smiled at Miss Zadie and stowed my bags.

"POSH seating, here we come." I said as we walked into the aerostat.

"Mudd?" Miss Zadie questioned, "This is the first time I get to tag along on your exploits; I guess I have a lot to learn."

"Not at all, we merely introduced Miss Riley to Mr. Muddly. The two of them worked twenty feet apart and never spoke to one another because they had not been introduced. Now, they are quite happy together. That's all there is to it." I smiled and walked toward the corridor.

"Winthrop, perhaps you need to…" Miss Zadie began.

I stopped in the corridor and turned 'round, "I am quite certain that you were in no way going to suggest that I become romantically involved! This is not even a glimmer of an idea in my life. Now, nothing more of this and off to our snuggery we go." I turned back around and walked to our seating area.

Chance chuckled as we sat down, "Thou wast ever an obstinate heretic in the despite of beauty. I shall see you 'ere I die, look pale with love… Shakespeare."

"With anger, with sickness, or with hunger, my lord; not with love." I smiled, "Ol' Willie would chortle at us both."

"Indeed, yet friendship is constant in all other things save in the office and affairs of love." Chance said.

"My good friend, where on Earth would love be able to find me long enough to fall for any woman? I prefer the smell of brandy to that of perfume and I am far too fond of my glass to put my lips against anything else. Adventure is my mistress and I shall not give that up for merely a woman who will warm my bed." I retorted.

Miss Zadie wrinkled her brow, "A woman to warm your bed!?"

Chance looked at her and then at me, "Now you've done it."

"A woman is not just a toy for you to 'warm your bed'! She is your partner, your confidante, your help-mate, not just some invisible baldric in which you… hang your bugle! Winthrop, if I ever hear you speak of a woman in such a way again, I shall teach you a lesson you will never forget." Miss Zadie was a bit cross with me.

"I merely meant that love was not for me." I back peddled.

She was still cross, "I know perfectly well what you meant. You, Dr. Corbyn, should be ashamed of yourself." She turned and looked out the window.

"Winnie, I would ask you not to upset my wife. This could now be a very, quiet trip." Chance looked out the window as well.

I now felt as though I had ruined the mood for everyone. The airship rose into the air and set off toward the Atlantic. Chance was right, it was very quiet for a while and then…

"Was that thunder?" I questioned.

Chance pointed out the front-most window, "Indeed it was. Look."

I turned where I could see. Our vessel wasn't very high above the ocean and there were definitely heading into a gale of some sort.

The stewardess was walking by, "Miss Riley, are we going into that storm? Shouldn't we go around it?" I inquired.

"It's okay, Dr. Corbyn. The storm will not distress our trip in the airship. We will fight the wind a bit, but for the most part, you will notice the rain on the windows and the lightning and thunder outside." Riley smiled at me.

"The lightning won't strike us will it?" I was still a bit nervous.

"No, Dr. Corbyn. Everything will be fine." She smiled at me and walked on.

"I hope the brandy will be coming soon." I muttered.

"Oh, now you want a woman to bring you brandy." Miss Zadie growled.

"Miss Zadie, this is not reasonable at all. I am obviously never going to fall in love and therefore, these things will never be an issue in my life. I would assume that Chance warms your… bed as much as you warm his and that is fine for the two of you, but I am in no need of having my… bed warmed. I would never go so far as to ask a woman to share my life, but I have no disrespect for women in any way." I wrinkled my brow as well.

A smile almost begrudgingly, crept onto her face, "I, too, shall see you 'ere I die, look pale with love."

I couldn't help laughing out loud, "Chance, your lady is wonderful."

Chance didn't reply. He was staring out the window as if he were looking at a ghost.

"What is it, Chance?" I looked out as well.

"There is something out there." He stood and walked toward the window.

In the far distance, I could see a blue glow. The lightning flashed and I could almost make out the shape of another airship.

"Plusterpot, it's too dark to see what it is." Chance looked back at me, "What do you make of it, Winnie?"

I stared a bit harder and the lightning flashed again. For a brief moment, I could see a red and black dirigible with two balloons and what looked like an old pirate ship hanging underneath. I knew instantly what it was, "Von Duggery!" I said aloud.

"What? Are you sure?" Miss Zadie was a bit unsettled now.

"The blue glow is his propulsion tubes and there is no mistaking the red and black of the Von Duggery family airship, The Domination. I only hope he doesn't know we are on this airship or he will try to end us all." I looked down at her.

"I am guessing he knows. The Domination is inching closer to us. There are thirty cannon on that vessel and a steel spine to attack other airships. What's our next move, Winnie?" Chance looked into my eyes.

"You go tell the Captain he's coming for us and I will figure some way to evade him." I moved toward the hold.

Chance ran to the front and told the Captain what was going on, "That blue glow is another airship and it is about to attack this ship."

"Poppycock, there are no pirates out this far." The Captain was not convinced.

"He's not a pirate, he's a thief without doubt, but he is not just a pirate. He wants nothing more than for us to never reach New York." Chance explained, "He has thirty cannon and a jagged metal spire to rip this balloon to shreds."

"I shall move up into the clouds and see if we can loose him." The Captain ordered the ship up into the storm clouds.

I walked in just in time with Mudd at my side, "Very good Captain. Now, everyone put out all the lights on this ship. He has to loose sight of us. Mudd, you take the back of the ship. Chance and I will handle the center; Captain, you and your men handle the front."

"On my way." Mudd replied.

"Agreed, Dr. Corbyn." The Captains said and a moment later, all the lights were out. The Captain bellowed out, "All stop! We'll let the blaggard fly right on by."

We felt the engines stop and the wind blow us sideways. Miss Zadie, Chance and I stood looking out the window. The cloud beside us began to glow with a bit of blue and then, the metal spire of The Domination ripped through the cloud.

Chapter 2

The Unimaginable Wealth In the Eye of the Moon

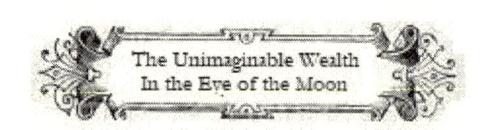

The airship was rising just as we were when we entered the cloud. The Domination rose as it neared us. The Captain dropped us a bit and The Domination skimmed the top of our balloon and never knew we were there.

It wasn't long and the Captain had us on a new course to New York and was back with us in POSH seating, "You two are always being chased by someone when you are on my ship! Why can't we just have a calm flight and arrive at our destination unscathed?" As the lights came on, he noticed Miss Zadie, "I apologize, Miss, I didn't realize there was a chaperone for them this time, but all the same; my ship is always in danger when these two are aboard."

"I completely understand, Captain. I am married to one of them and there is always difficulty in their general approximation. I will try to keep them under control for the remainder of the trip, however, I do suggest that you watch for that other dirigible, as it has onboard a man who is rather wicked and would steal your ship from you and tell everyone that you gave it to him because you adored him so." Miss Zadie gave the Captain a look that would back down a cobra.

He stammered a moment and the finally got out, "Yes, yes Ma'am, I will do that. Thank you Ma'am." And he was off to the bridge.

Miss Zadie then turned the "look" on me, "Miss Zadie, why loose your venom on me? I merely stopped Von Duggery from seeing us escape."

The "look" slowly changed into a smile, "Works every time."

"Plusterpot! Miss Zadie, you got me. I blusterly well thought you were about to pounce." I couldn't help but chuckle at myself.

"Yes, I see that look all the time. Now, how in the blusterly bell do we get into New York without that pirate sending us to the drink?" Chance didn't look very calm at all.

Miss Zadie put her hand on his, "He went north and we went south. Everything will be fine."

We spent the next couple of days watching out the window for other airships, but the rest of the trip was uneventful. We arrived about an hour and a half late and began to maneuver into an aero dock.

Suddenly, another airship appeared and slammed against ours, knocking it out of place and forcing the Captain to move to another aero dock tie-down. We all knew it had to be Von Duggery.

Miss Riley came and told us we could disembark and Mudd gave us our bags as we exited.

Chance and I exited and walked to the bottom of the platform. We were looking about when The Domination, "accidently" fired a harpoon into the side of the airship we had just left.

I was about to use an exclamation, but I heard, "Plusterpot! What the blusterly bell was that?" From behind me.

I knew the voice. I turned slowly to see Miss Zadie talking to the loveliest creature I had ever seen, "For the love of cumquats, if it isn't Miss Charlotte Wolf, as I live and breathe."

"Hello, Dub." Miss Charlotte smiled at me.

"Dub? Charlee, do you two know one another?" Miss Zadie asked.

Miss Charlotte looked at Miss Zadie, "Heavens, yes. This is the only man, other than my father, to call me Charlotte and live to tell about it. I just like the way he says it."

Chance looked at me questioningly, "Dub?"

"My initials, ol' boy, W.C., of course. Miss Charlotte always shortened it to 'Dub'. You're looking at the only person in the world who can shoot the Gov'ner better than I." I smiled at Miss Charlotte.

"You still have that ol' peashooter of an elephant gun?" She smiled back.

"Indeed, though I have not brought it on this trip. In fact, I have not any weapons at all." I walked toward her.

Miss Charlotte was a very lovely woman. She wore her straight, blonde hair back in a tail under her large, American hat. She had on a frilly white blouse with a green and black corset on top of that. On her hip was a dark brown gun belt with an unusual revolver on either side. Her trousers were black and grey stripped and her longcoat or duster, as she always called it, was brown leather. She had a huge silver belt buckle as well. Her eyes were blue… almost robin's egg blue and her skin was 'seasoned' from the western sky.

Miss Charlotte grabbed me and we hugged for a moment, we hadn't seen one another in many years.

Miss Zadie looked at us, "Charlee, how do you two know each other?"

Miss Charlotte stepped back, "Dub and I use to hang about together at the University. We were partners in some of the digs in archeology. I had quite the flutters for this young man."

I know I blushed, but I couldn't help it. I wanted to say something manly and charming, but all that came out was, "I was quite fluttery, as well."

Chance laughed aloud, "Fluttery? I think you're fluttering right now. Come on W.C., let's go find the Anasazi."

I looked into Miss Charlotte's eyes and then walked back down to retrieve my baggage, "Miss Charlotte, how long will it take to get us to these dwellings."

"I thought you'd never ask. We'll take a train to Denver and then my Desert Skiff from there. Should be just a few days." She explained.

"Desert Skiff?" I remembered our ride with Sheldon across the deserts outside Cairo.

"I'll show ya when we get there." Miss Charlotte smiled.

I noticed a look of annoyance on Chance's face as he was looking over my shoulder. Then, I heard a voice, a greasy, crackly voice, "Well, Dr. Corbyn. I see you are still a second class archeologist and your taste in friends is still as droll as ever."

I turned around to see Morley Von Duggery. He was very thin and wore a black suit with a black top hat. He had an oily handlebar mustache and a small, scruffy beard. He stood there smiling with his lips spread apart, and all of his gnarled teeth showing, "Hello Duggie. Stole anything worthwhile lately?"

"My name's not Duggie, It's Von Duggery, you old windbag. You might as well pack it up now. I will have a jump on you getting to the treasure. You know I will win." His voice made my teeth grind against one another.

One of his workers came around the dock, "Sir, we can't get the harpoon out of the other ship. And the port detective says we are grounded until he can look into the incident."

Von Duggery threw his hands in the air, "Must I do everything." He stormed off following the other gentleman.

I looked at Miss Charlotte, "Can we get there faster than him?" I asked.

Miss Charlotte had a scowl on her face as well, "If I have to ride a white buffalo, I'll get us there faster."

"I see you remember Von Duggery as well." I noted aloud.

"Yeah, I remember him stealing our discovery down the hill from Stonehenge. Most cantankerous wicker fuggly to ever slither in the dirt." Her scowl worsened.

I looked at Miss Zadie, "You see? Wicker fugglies."

Chance laughed, "Well, you two wicker fuggly despisers, what's our next move?"

I looked at Miss Charlotte, "Do you have a faster way across this land than his bag of hot air?"

"What we have is direction. I know where these places are and he will have to find them." She explained.

"There is more than one?" Miss Zadie asked.

"Oh, my yes. The pictures mostly came from the palace." Miss Charlotte was getting giddy now.

"The palace? They had a palace?" I questioned.

"No, that's just what I call it, The Cliff Palace. It's very large and quite lovely, but we best be goin' if we're gonna make that train." Miss Charlotte turned and walked toward the bottom of the platform.

The rest of us began walking down to follow. Suddenly there was a loud "POP" and the sound of rushing air, "Sounds like Duggie got his harpoon back." Chance smiled.

A moment later, "Ya blasted idiot! Look at the hole ya put in me ship. If I had a cannon, I'd blow a hole in your side just as big." The captain of our transport was quite upset.

"I have cannon and I'll finish the job if you don't shut that obnoxious hole in your face." Von Duggery hissed.

"You have cannon on board?" Another voice piped in.

"Yes, I do and who the bricker brack are you?" Von Duggery asked.

"I'm the port inspector. I'm afraid you're in violation of at least ten statutes already and I haven't even begun my investigations, yet." The inspector's voice rang out loud and clear.

"How long is this poppycock going to take? I have places to go?" Von Duggery was still quite haughty.

"If I put my mind to it, I should have you out of here in…oh… best guess, I'd say three days." The inspector was in earnest, of that there was no doubt.

"Three days? I won't stand for it! I have places that I have to be. The British Archeology Society will hear of this! I'll have your badge!" We walked off laughing, listening to Von Duggery rant to no avail.

"I believe we have plenty of time to take the train now." Miss Charlotte laughed and looked into my eyes, "I'm glad to see you again, Dub." She realized what she had said, "And you, too, Zadie, and you Chance." A smile curled up on her lovely face, "Let's go have an adventure!"

"Adventure, indeed." I felt the same smile curl around my face. Miss Charlotte slid her arm under mine and we walked across the aero-docks to the train station.

Our train was actually waiting on our arrival, as Miss Charlotte had asked them earlier. We climbed aboard and hadn't even stowed our baggage before the train lurched into motion.

I noticed that there were three or four gentlemen who ran to catch the train as it began to move. It struck me funny that the train had been waiting for us and yet there were other parties who arrived after us.

"Chance, why would these other gentlemen be running after the train? Was the train not waiting for our arrival?" I pondered aloud.

"That's a good question. Perhaps I should ask the conductor." Chance said as we moved into the seating area.

We sat down and waited for the conductor to come through. I looked at the seat across from me, "Miss Charlotte, I noticed a boot-toe shaped picket fence on the front of the engine. What on earth is that for?"

She thought for a moment, "You mean the cattle scoop? Ya see, out in the West, cattle roam free on the ranches and the buffalo roam wherever they please, what's left of them anyway. The tracks go through wherever they need to. The scoop is designed to scoop an animal off the track and away from the engine, thus preventing damage to the train and hopefully the animal as well."

I looked out the window, "When will we be in 'the West'?" I asked.

"As soon as you cross the Mighty Mississippi." Miss Charlotte put her hand on my knee, "You'll know when you're in the West. It's my country."

I looked at my knee and then into her eyes once again, "Your country? You mean it's wild and beautiful?"

Chance smiled and whispered, "Nice one, Winnie."

Miss Charlotte blushed, "It is wild and beautiful, but I mean that's where I grew up and I love being out there. I am so excited to share it with you as you shared so much of your country with me."

I could feel Chance and Miss Zadie looking at me. I knew I had said that I didn't have time for a woman and I was certain they were confused by my... friendship with Miss Charlotte, but I was quite sure that our relationship was nothing more than two old friends off on an adventure together.

"I have to admit, Miss Charlotte, I probably didn't study the American natives nearly as well as I should have. There just wasn't enough published about them." I smiled.

The train rattled and blew its whistle at every crossing. Miss Charlotte looked out the window, "You're so right, Dub, we white folk treated these people with so much disrespect and were down right murderous to them. Now that we have them all corralled on reservations, we are starting to see that there was so much history that we just wiped out." She looked back at me, "The Anasazi may have been running from our influence or even been subject to explorers looking for Eldorado. The adobe buildings on the cliffs look as if they were made of gold in the setting sun."

"Do we have any evidence of that?" I asked.

"None whatsoever, but it is a possibility. The Explorers were quite often lost. Their maps were vague and halfhearted." Miss Charlotte looked out the window again.

The Conductor came by for our tickets, "Tickets please."

Miss Charlotte handed him our tickets, "Here ya go, my friend."

"Very, good ma'am. I see the gentlemen will have berth A4 and the ladies will have berth B4. Those will be through the door at the back, into the next car." The Conductor explained.

"A and B stand for...?" I stammered.

"A is 'Above' and B is 'Below', sir." He grinned.

"Bully, I get the upper!" I liked the upper berth, obviously.

"That means I have to sleep with you rather than my wife and you snore like a banshee." Chance smiled then looked at the Conductor, "Who were the gentlemen who ran for the train after it started moving?"

"There were no available spaces left on this train. No one should have jumped on after we started moving." He looked angry.

"They grabbed on the last car, my good man." I explained and he darted off to the back of the train.

"Well, shall we talk about our findings thus far?" Miss Charlotte began.

"Of course, Charlee. What I got deciphered before the tintypes were stolen was that they had to hide their wealth from some sort of marauders and is hidden in the eye of the moon. The

39

large tintype said that only the sun through the heart of the Thunderbird will find its way to the eye of the moon." Miss Zadie explained.

"Von Duggery bamboozled the tintypes didn't he?" Miss Charlotte smiled.

"Yes, Charlee, I am so sorry." Miss Zadie felt so bad for loosing them.

"No problem, I still have the originals." She smiled at me, "I'm not sure about the thunderbird heart part, but the eye of the moon could be a reflection in a pool or basin of water."

"Of course, it would look like an eye during a full moon." I smiled. I, too, loved unfolding the mysteries of the past.

"Now how does the sun look through a thunderbird? If the thunderbird is there, the sun will be behind the clouds." Miss Charlotte continued.

"Perhaps, it doesn't mean an actual thunderstorm. For instance, perhaps there is a large drawing of a thunderbird that you can only see in the daylight." I offered an explanation.

"I see what yer sayin', but how does the sun pass through its heart?" She asked.

"I'm not sure, but I think…" My words were interrupted by a large ruckus in the back of the train.

I looked at Chance. He shrugged his shoulders. That's when we heard the conductor's voice ring out, "You ever jump my train again and I'll fill ya full of buckshot!"

Chance looked out the window at the three tumbling bodies trying to stand up and run away. He started laughing, "They appeared to be Duggie's henchmen."

"Got their comeuppance, I'd say." Miss Charlotte laughed along.

I watched the angry Conductor walk back through the car, "Indeed, they did, I'd say, indeed they did."

Chapter 3

The Unimaginable Wealth
In the Eye of the Moon

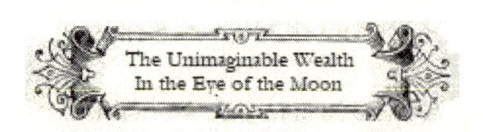

As the day went on, we stopped at towns and cities here and there. Chance and I were careful to watch who got on, in the event that Von Duggery sent more adversaries.

We crossed endless rivers and I would ask, "Is this the Mississippi?"

Miss Charlotte would smile, "No, you'll know when you cross the Mighty Mississippi." She was so right.

Our train began to cross what appeared to be a long skinny lake, but was in fact, a huge, muddy river. The water seemed to be moving as fast as the train, but the river had to be deep. There were whirlpools and eddies everywhere and yet sandbars built up here and there from all the soil being brought down its course, "This is the Mississippi." I looked into Miss Charlotte's eyes.

"It is, Dub, welcome to the West." She smiled at me. I felt as though she had brought me into a secret passage leading to the biggest treasure I could ever imagine. I was now part of her world; A world which she had prepared just for my adventure.

We traveled a while more and then the land grew flat and wide, "Goodness, it's like an ocean of grass." I commented.

"This is where the buffalo used to roam in massive herds." Miss Charlotte looked out across the waves of green, "They are mostly gone now." The sorrow in her voice was quite evident.

"Yes, I heard they were hunted for sport and for their skins into extinction. A sad state, I must say." I tried to express my feelings, but it is not something that I'm good at.

Chance looked out, "This isn't where we will find cliff dwellings, is it?"

Charlotte looked at him, "No, no it's not. We have to travel across the great prairie before we get into the Rockies."

"But if this is where they hunted buffalo for meat, why is it so far from them?" He questioned.

"Oh, Chance, buffalo used to roam from the Appalachians to the Rockies. They filled this land with life and helped the prairie become as fertile as it is." Miss Charlotte was quite an authority on these buffalo.

Miss Zadie looked at Miss Charlotte, "Didn't the Anasazi learn to farm?"

"Indeed they did. This became the first order of feeding themselves. Their farms were ever so important. They learned to dry and store grain and make it last for winter after winter." She was a bit giddy once again.

"How does one farm in the mountains? Wouldn't the prairie be a better place to live if you are a farmer?" Miss Zadie asked.

"They farmed on the top of plateaus and in fertile valleys. They avoided the flatlands because of other tribes who would raid their lands and take their food without working the land for themselves. Thieves and marauders would filch an entire season of work and be gone." Miss Charlotte was adamant when it came to the plights of people being taken advantage of. I remembered that from school.

"Tell me something, what form of money did they use?" I asked Miss Charlotte.

"Money? They had no need of money. They were a group of people who lived together and worked for the good of the group. There was no need for bartering of any kind. If Miss Ellie needed a new basket, but she wasn't good at weaving, then Miss Mabel would weave her one and Miss Ellie would use the basket to gather grain to feed the group including Miss Mabel. It was as simple as that." She explained.

"So where does the wealth of an unimaginable size come into play?" I was now unsure of what we were looking for.

"Well, that's the question of the day, isn't it? I would imagine it would be grain or perhaps gold that they found in the mountains which they could trade to other tribes for things they wanted, but didn't necessarily need. For all we know, the wealth could actually be Eldorado, the city of gold. The Anasazi may be ancestors of the Inca and Aztecs." Miss Charlotte was giddy once again and so was Miss Zadie. They giggled together like they were talking about men.

"I will be quite excited to see these dwellings." I interrupted their merriment.

"I can't wait to get you to the Canyon of the Ancients. It's like our Valley of the Kings. There is evidence of native people there from as far back as the ice age." Miss Charlotte looked into my eyes and smiled.

"Bully! I can't wait to see this for myself." I smiled back.

Suddenly there was an explosion on the north side of the train, "Plusterpot! What was that?" I shouted as we all looked out the window.

Then there was another blast out the south side of the train, "That is cannon fire!" Chance said as he jumped up, "Quick, Winnie, we have to do something."

"Are there pirate out here in the west?" I asked Miss Charlotte.

"Bandits maybe, but they would be on horseback. There wouldn't be cannons." She replied.

Chance and I looked at one another and all four of us said in unison, "Von Duggery!"

Chance and I hastened to the last car of the train. Sure enough, there was the Domination following along the tracks shooting at our train.

Miss Zadie and Miss Charlotte showed up behind us, "Winnie, you didn't bring that elephant gun and we could sure use it right about now."

"Indeed, if they hit this train or the tracks, everyone onboard could be killed." I exclaimed. I reached into my pocket and pulled out my scope, "There are two powder kegs on deck. One next to the gentlemen firing that blasted cannon; the other is in the back next to the rail and the…" I looked at Chance and smiled, "The rigging."

I turned and looked at Miss Charlotte, "My dear, are you as proficient with those weapons as you are with the Gov'ner?" I said pointing at the revolvers on the hips.

I cannon blast hit just behind us to the left as the corners of her mouth turned up, "I am, Dup, even more so. Show me where I'm aimin' and we'll shut down those cannon."

I pointed out the small barrel next to the rigging holding the ship under the steam-filled balloon, "If you can hit that barrel, it will cut the rigging holding the ship up straight and he will have to land and make repairs."

Miss Charlotte pulled both revolvers. She turned the cylinder on one, "I only keep three bullets in this one." She smiled and took aim. They went off at the same time and she made a direct hit. The back of the ship dropped just as the cannon fired and the cannon ball went straight up through the balloon. The back of the ship hit the ground and then the front. In moments, the ship was sliding across the prairie grass. It came to a stop and the balloon settled down over the top of the ship like a blanket.

From the muffled ship and just above the sound of the train, we heard, "Corbyn! I'll get you for this!"

We all started laughing, "That was an amazing shot, Miss Charlotte." I said as we started walking back to our seats.

The Conductor appeared in our path, "You folks alright? What in the name of soot was that all about?" He was both concerned and angry.

"We're all fine, thanks to Miss Charlotte, here. She made short work of those pirates." I smiled at her.

"Pirates, following a train? What kind of hogwash is that? I have a mind to toss you all of this train. We don't throw explosives off the caboose. I won't stand for it." He hissed.

"Throw… explosives… are you a ninny. We saved your train from certain derailment and you… you…" I became furious.

"Dub, in a way, it is our fault. Von Duggery is trying to stop us from getting there first." Miss Charlotte made me feel calm.

I took a breath, "We shall endeavor not to be a problem to you for the rest of the trip."

"See that you're not, not any of ya." The Conductor turned and hastened up the aisle.

"Well, that was exciting." Chance smiled at me.

"Which part, the cannons, the airship falling from the sky or the scolding we got for saving the train?" I sneered.

"All of them, I should say. Remember, Winnie, no good deed goes unpunished." Chance chortled and walked passed me heading for his seat.

Miss Zadie smiled, "Winthrop, you have very fast reflexes and your mind works quickly, but Charlee is a better shot."

"Indeed, my dear, indeed. I may need to pick up a revolver like hers." I looked at Miss Charlotte's hips.

"Colt 45s. Best pistol ever made. I can shoot the fly off a bullfrog's tongue at thirty yards." She put her hands on her pistols and looked at me, "Might have to get you one." She thought for a moment, "And a Stetson; that pith helmet does nothing for your hansom face and that lovely beard."

I looked back at her, "Stetson?"

"Best hat money can buy. I think maybe a ten gallon hat might work with that lovely buckskin duster o' yers." Miss Charlotte smiled at me again.

"Buckskin duster? Oh, my longcoat. Wild Bill Hickok gave this to me after I saved his life in New York. He thought my brown longcoat was unflattering and exchanged it for his." I explained.

"You saved Wild Bill's life? How did that happen?" She asked.

"He was there on the street talking with some of us about Deadwood, South Dakota and a runaway trolley was headed right for him. I grabbed him and throw him to the side and jumped myself just in time. He rolled over with his revolver in his hand and then saw the trolley. He looked at me and started laughing. He thanked me and traded coats with me." I had not told that story for quite some time.

"Wild Bill was an icon out here." Miss Charlotte looked down at her boots.

"Was? Has he passed?" I asked.

"Yep, he was shot during a game of cards. The hand he was playing has now become known as 'the dead man's hand'." She looked back into my eyes.

"The dead man's hand? What was it?" I inquired.

"A pair of aces and a pair of eights." Miss Charlotte tried to smile.

"I think we should move toward our seats, now" Miss Zadie suggested.

I took my eyes away for Miss Charlotte's, "Oh, um, yes. Yes, quite right."

Miss Charlotte turned around and walked up the aisle. I watched her walk. I enjoy the way she moves. Miss Zadie slapped me on the shoulder, "Winthrop, shame on you. Now go."

I was caught unaware, "What? Oh, yes, of course." I set off following Miss Charlotte.

Miss Charlotte sat down and I waited for Miss Zadie and then sat across from Miss Charlotte once again.

Chance looked at Miss Zadie, "My love, what was the symbol you couldn't identify on the tintypes?"

"Symbol? You mean the size of the wealth? Well, it said that it was bigger than everything the moon shines on or its light touches. I don't understand what that would mean." She explained.

"What was the symbol for the moon?" Miss Charlotte asked.

"It was a circle with lines underneath each one getting bigger than the one before it." Miss Zadie said.

"Are you sure it wasn't an oval?" Miss Charlotte asked.

"Maybe, why?" Miss Zadie asked.

53

"A circle with lines pointing away is the sun; a circle with no lines is the moon, but an oval with lines under it is the thoughts or dreams of a man. Perhaps it was saying that the wealth was bigger than a man could think or imagine."

"So, we are talking about the unimaginable wealth hidden in the eye of the moon?" I questioned.

"That would be my take on it." Miss Charlotte smiled.

"How do we get to the eye of the moon?" Miss Zadie thought out loud.

"First we have to find out what the eye of the moon is and then find out where it is." Miss Charlotte was quite practical.

We all sat quiet for a bit and thought about what we were in for. The search could take months, even years. Then again, it might come up as plain as the nose on one's face. Either way, we were all in for quite an adventure.

I had to wonder how bad Von Duggery's ship was damaged and how soon we were going to have to deal with his treachery once again. I didn't wish for anyone to be harmed, but I did wish he would just pack it in and go home. I knew that would never be the case, but it would make this adventure much more enjoyable.

The next day we pulled into Denver. The air was thin and hard to breath, but we were a mile into the air. Miss Charlotte smiled, "You'll get used to the air in a few days. Come on, Dub, let's find you that hat."

I followed along as did Chance and Miss Zadie. They were holding hands, it was quite revolting. I did my best to catch Miss Charlotte, "I was thinking…" I was out of breath.

Miss Charlotte stopped, "What was that, Dub?"

"I was thinking… I need to… get a revolver." I said between breaths.

"You want a hogleg? Perfect place to get one is the same outfitter who has the Stetsons I was thinking about." She turned back around and started walking again.

"Hogleg? Yes, well, I didn't bring any weapons with me. After the fiasco on the train, I thought it best if I picked something up." I listened to her boots on the brick walkway. "Do they make those boots for men?" I asked.

"Yes sir, same outfitter." Miss Charlotte turned into a huge building and we all followed.

The inside was even more enormous that the outside. Chance and Miss Zadie began looking at clothes as well, I presume to fit in with the western surrounding. Miss Charlotte walked me over to the gun case. "Amazing, there are all kinds of revolvers."

"Sir, here we call them 'pistols' or 'six shooters'. Is there one in particular you'd like to see?" The gentleman behind the counter appeared to be quite knowledgeable.

"This young lady referred to a hogleg. Is there one of those in your case?" I looked at him.

"That's just another reference to a pistol. These are all hoglegs. I would suggest a Colt 45 to match the young lady's." He was a very smooth talking salesman.

A few minutes later, I had a six shooter strapped around my waist Miss Charlotte had me in a pair of what she called "cowboy boots", "Now Dub, let's put you in a Stetson."

We walked over to a huge rack of hats. There were hats of every shape and size, toppers, bowlers and hats similar to Miss Charlottes, "Good heavens, which one do you suggest?" I looked at Miss Charlotte.

She reached over and picked up one and set it on my head. She looked at it a moment, then took it off and put her fist up inside. The design in the top popped out and made a rounded top like a derby and then she sat it back on my head, "Nope, not a ten gallon person…" She paused and looked at me, "I see the one." She walked over and picked up a short, black hat and then walked back to me.

"My dear, I don't were black. It gets too hot." She slid the hat on my head. It fit beautifully.

Chance and Miss Zadie walked up behind me, "Winnie, that hat is amazing. I think you finally found a hat to replace that plusterpot pith helmet."

Miss Zadie smiled, "You look very hansom, Winthrop."

Miss Charlotte pointed to a mirror. I stepped over and looked in. The hat was flat on top with a slight indent. It had a large brim and a silver hatband with a blue-green stone set every few inches. It went with my longcoat quite well, "I'll take it." I was pleased with the way I looked.

Miss Charlotte smiled and walked over, "I think you look perfect. The hat works perfectly with your beard." She ran her fingers through my beard.

I suddenly became flustered, "Yes, well, thank you. I um, I mean, we should be off. I uh, yes." I couldn't seem top take my eyes off of hers.

"Come on, Winnie, you've had enough poppycock for one trip." Chance looked cross.

Chapter 4

The Unimaginable Wealth In the Eye of the Moon

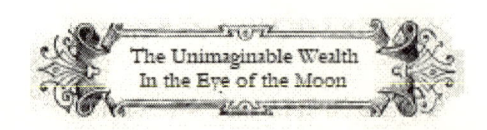

Chance gave me that look of "You are making a fool of yourself". I shook my head, "Yes, quite enough. Where is this transportation of yours?" I asked Miss Charlotte.

"Oh, yes it's this way." She paid for my new hat and walked toward the door.

Miss Zadie slugged Chance in the arm, "You stop interfering or I'll starch your skivvies again."

I turned around, "Interfering in what?"

Miss Zadie took her husband's arm, "Nothing Winthrop." And they walked out behind Miss Charlotte.

I followed and soon was listening to the sound of Miss Charlotte's boots, but this time they were accompanied by the sound of my own. In a moment, we were in perfect synchronization. I found that I was right next to her as we walked toward our destination.

Miss Charlotte seemed to be a bit upset. She wouldn't say a word, "Miss Charlotte, is everything alright?" No answer was forthcoming. "I am dreadfully sorry if I have done something to upset you. I do seem to get flustered around you and my words seem to come out askew."

Miss Charlotte stopped and looked right into my eyes, "Do you want to have this adventure with me or not?"

Even though she was angry, her eyes pierced me through the heart, "Indeed I do; more than anything."

"Then we are partners. I am not your assistant!" She growled. She looked back at Chance, "You; don't you throw 'poppycock' at me after the years you chased Zadie while I was trying to be with my friend. Dub and I are good friends and if we want to frolic in poppycock, that's none of your affair!" She whirled back around and began walking again.

I looked at Chance. He had a glassy look in his eye. Miss Zadie had a grin on her face a mile wide. I turned back around and tried to catch up with Miss Charlotte, "Miss… Charlotte…"

She slowed down and looked at me as I caught up to her, "Dub, I like you a lot. I don't want you to make light of that. I have liked you since the day you spilled the mummy out on the desk in class. You are funny and cute and you don't think of yourself as better than me. Please don't change that so you don't look bad in front of your friend."

"Miss Charlotte, I have liked you since you first shot The Gov'ner. I am grateful that you think I'm funny; I can't imagine how you see me as cute, but I have always seen you as one of the best things to ever happen to me. I am not better than you. In point of fact, it is you who are better. I'm just me." I tried to smile.

Miss Charlotte stopped, "I think we are better together… as a team." A tiny smile crept across her face, "Now, would you please stop calling me Charlotte? Call me Charlee. I really don't like Charlotte."

I smiled, "Of course Miss Charl… Miss Charlee."

She started laughing, "Well that's closer." She turned and walked back to the train station.

"Charlee, we are back at the train station." I pointed out.

"Yep. The Desert Skiff is on the far side." She said as she walked around the corner.

I walked around the corner and there was a very familiar sight, "Miss… Charlee, that looks just like Sheldon's craft but with a top."

"Of course. He showed me how to build one and the top is for the cloudbursts." She explained. The machine was amazing; the bottom looked like a steam engine with no firebox nor boiler. There was a large glass bowl with a lid. There were pipes coming out of the lid and entering the machine.

There was a box on top of that with five seats in it and a shaft going up through the cloudburst cover with four 'flower pedal' shaped arms at the top, each nearly twelve feel long. A second shaft went from side to side at the back of the box.

Chance and Miss Zadie walked around the corner, "Shelly is here?" Chance thought the same thing I did.

"No, ol' man. Charlee built this one, but it looks just like Sheldon's does it not?" I was a bit taken aback.

Miss Zadie smiled and whispered, "Charlee?"

"She asked me to call her Charlee. She doesn't like Charlotte any more than I like Winnie." I glared at Chance who has always called me Winnie knowing I despise it.

"Hop on. Let's get this adventure in the air." Charlee said as she climbed the ladder.

We all climbed on board and a moment later I could hear the steam rising in the tubes. The ship began to move and we were off through the mountains. I say "through" as we were staying in valleys rather than trying to go over the mountains. I assume that was for breathing purposes as we were having a hard time breathing as it was, less air might have been intolerable.

"We are going to spend the night in a little town in the Arkansas valley. Salida is her name." Charlee yelled back over the sound of the machinery.

"Isn't salida Spanish for 'the way out'?" Miss Zadie asked.

"Yes, it is. Salida is the way out of the valley." Charlee smiled, "I know some of the people in town and there are several Ute guides who know The Valley of the Ancients and possibly where the tintypes were taken."

A few hours later, the sun was beginning to set behind the Rocky Mountains and we were flying just above the Arkansas River. There were rock walls on either side of the valley and we seemed to be getting closed in upon.

Just as it was getting uncomfortable, we came out into a lovely little valley with a lovely little town in it. There was a small train station and a smelter stack nearby. I couldn't help but think we were suddenly in an American west cow town. Charlee set the skiff down near the hotel and we all climbed down.

"Miss… I mean Charlee, does your skiff have a name? All good craft do, you know." I smiled.

Charlee smiled over her shoulder, "Indeed she does. It's a word I learned from you actually. It means cantankerous. Can you guess?"

I thought for a minute and remembered fussing about a professor to Charlee when we were on a dig, "I have it."

"So, what is the name of my skiff?" She giggled.

"The Bilious. Named for Professor McNair." I was pleased with myself.

"Yep, and she is just about as bilious as the professor." Charlee walked into the hotel, "My good sir, we need three rooms." She looked back at Chance and Miss Zadie, "I assume you two love bird are fine with sleeping in the same bed."

Miss Zadie smiled and looked up at her husband who was uncharacteristically speechless and veiled in a very prominent blush. I had no alternative but to laugh aloud, "Chance, she zinged you. You're as red as…" I was stopped short by my friend.

"As red as what, Winnie, as your face has been this whole trip? You've been head over heels and we all know it. You need to get your head out of … wherever it is and get it back on to our work!" Chance snapped at me like a serpent.

I stood there silent for a moment and then turned to Charlee, "Three rooms will be fine."

Charlee looked at me and then at Chance, "I didn't mean no disrespect, Chance. I just meant you two are married and you could share a room. I am sorry."

I refused to turn 'round as it would mean facing the others. The entire trip was running through my mind and I could see how foolish I had been acting. I was most taken by Charlee, but I "haven't the time nor the inclination for such falderal and balderdash" if I remember my own words.

Chance finally spoke, "You did nothing wrong, Charlee. It is I who should apologize. My friend, Winthrop has never been married and has yet to experience such things. He did nothing more than point out my blush and I attacked him ever so savagely. I hope he will accept my apology."

I don't think Chance had called me Winthrop since we were kids. I slowly turned 'round and Chance was looking at me with a very somber look on his face, "Chin up ol' man, you called me

Winthrop; there's hope for you yet. Now, let's get to our rooms so we can continue our adventure."

The man at the desk looked at me, "Y'all are a strange bunch of travelers, I gotta say. Where are ya from?"

Charlee answered, "I'm from Texas, but my friends here are from London. You may know this gentleman here; he's the Archeologist Extraordinaire Doctor Winthrop Corbyn!"

The gentleman behind the counter looked at me and then at Charlee, "He's the guy who found that tomb in Egypt?" Charlee nodded, "It's an honor, sir. The way you're dressed, I thought you were related to Wild Bill. Would you sign the guest book with your full title, please?"

"Indeed, my good man, I shall." I signed the guest book and he handed me a key. "You know, I saved Wild Bill's life in New York and he gave me his long coat."

"So you are his family, then, I thought the coat looked familiar." He smiled and handed the pen to Charlee. He looked down at her signature and spouted, "Goodness, are you *The* Charlee Wolf?"

"I'm the only one I know of. Do you know me?" Charlee was a bit confused.

"Everyone knows the Charlee Wolf who stood off the bandits who tried to hold up the D and RG (Denver and Rio Grande) gold train. You also saved the Ute kids who had fallen off that cliff. You're even more famous than Dr. Corbyn." He was giddy as a school… well, you understand, "Goodness, two famous people in one day." He looked at Chance, "And who are you? Are you famous, too? Wait, you two are brothers aren't you?" He nodded toward me.

Chance looked at me and a smirk came across his lips, "We're not brothers, we merely have the same haberdasher." This is something I have said for years when people would guess us as brothers. This is the first time Chance has ever said it.

Miss Zadie began to giggle as did Charlee. I blinked twice and cleared my throat, "Heavens to Betsy, Chance, that's my line."

Chance started laughing, "I know old friend, I know."

We all had a good laugh and headed for our rooms. Charlee stopped on the stairs and asked the clerk, "Do you know, are Whitetail or Bunny in town right now?"

"Bunny Stumpjump is out with another Englishman right now, but Whitetail is in the General Store helping out I believe." He answered.

"Another Englishman? Do you know who that would be?" I asked.

"Pennington was his name I believe. Someone you know?" The clerk replied.

"No, never heard of him. Just making sure it wasn't that snollygoster, Von Duggery." I gave a bit of a shudder.

"Snollygoster? Is that a new one?" Miss Zadie grinned at her husband.

Chance looked down at her, "No dear, snollygoster is actually an American word. It means a shifty, unscrupulous person; an oily wicker fuggly such as our old friend, Von Duggery."

"Oh, I like that one. Snollygoster." She smiled up at Chance as he was a bit taller than she.

"Let's get settled in and meet down here in half an hour. We'll eat and go see if Whitetail can take us where we need to go." Charlee said as she walked on up the stairs.

"Right-o" I agreed and we all proceeded to our rooms.

A bit later, I arrived downstairs to find I was the last one to do so, "How much did you pack along with you this time, ol' bean? We've been waiting forever." Chance gave me his classic smirk and Miss Zadie nudged him in the ribs.

"Chance, you know perfectly well that I always travel light." I retorted.

Charlee chuckled, "That's not the way I remember it, but you did only have two cases. I assume there is only so much you could have pressed into that."

"Where do we find Whitetail?" Miss Zadie asked.

"The general store or someplace where there are people in abundance. He likes to listen in on conversations." Charlee smiled.

"He eavesdrops on other people?" Miss Zadie was a bit shocked.

"Travelers think he's just an Indian and can't understand English. Fact is, he speaks English as well as you and me." Charlee chuckled again.

Charlee turned about and headed out the door. We all walked down the main street toward the general store. Suddenly Chance looked down, "Winnie! What's this shadow?"

We all looked up to see The Domination floating overhead. Men began dropping down on ropes and pulling her down toward us, "Plusterpot! It's Von Duggery! How on earth would he know where we were?" I hissed.

"Quick, into the general store. Maybe he doesn't know we are here yet." Charlee ran for the store.

We all ran and then peered out through the window. A few minutes later, Von Duggery slunk out of the depths of the airship. He had something in his hand. He walked to the saloon.

I could feel heat from behind me, "That snollygoster has my tintypes!" Miss Zadie was furious and began to walk outside.

Chance grabbed her, "Not now, love. We will get them back later."

"Man in cloudship not friend?" Came a deep voice from behind.

"Absolutely not!" I fussed as I turned about.

There stood a native, dressed all in buckskin. He had dark skin and long, black hair. Charlee turned 'round, "Whitetail, these folks know you speak English very well."

"Oh, very well then. So, who is the gentleman, for lack of a better word, in black?" Whitetail asked.

"His name is Von Duggery and he is a treasure seeking blaggard." Chance bellowed.

"Looking for the fountain of youth or Eldorado?" Whitetail asked jokingly.

"He has tintypes of images in The Valley of the Ancients. He took them from us and I think he thinks they lead to treasure, but if he would use his head, he would realize that treasure to one man is not to another." Charlee explained to her friend.

"What are the images?" White tail asked.

"They are etchings that tell of immeasurable or unspeakable wealth in the eye of the moon and that the sun must pass through the heart of the thunderbird." Miss Zadie told him.

"The ones, The Monkey Heckler took; I know where those came from." Whitetail said this in the most nonchalant way, as if everyone should know what a Monkey Heckler is.

Charlee looked at me and then back at Whitetail, "The Monkey Heckler?"

"Yes. David." He said.

Charlee chuckled, "Oh, David, I had forgotten the Monkey Heckler thing."

"He lives in the Valley of the Ancients and has taken most of the pictures from there." He smiled at Miss Zadie, "He's a bit eccentric, if you know what I mean." He thought for a moment and then said, "If this Von Duggery is looking for someone to take him into the valley, maybe I could pass as a guide who would be interested and get a look at the tintypes. Then I would know right where to take you and he would be none the wiser."

"We haven't even settled on a price, yet." Charlee said.

"I want one fifth of whatever we find. Not but an equal share." Whitetail smiled at Charlee.

"If we find nothing?" She asked.

He looked around at us, "I am quite sure we have enough talent to find something." He smiled and walked toward the saloon.

"I have a feeling that he knows more than he's letting on." Miss Zadie expressed.

"I was thinking the same thing." Charlee agreed.

Chapter 5

The Unimaginable Wealth In the Eye of the Moon

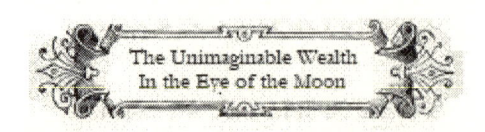

Moments later, a ruckus erupted in the saloon, "Stop him! He has my property!" Everyone could hear Von Duggery screeching.

Whitetail burst in the back door of the general store, handed the tintypes to Charlee and then darted on out the front. A moment later, five of Von Duggery's men were standing in front of Charlee, "'ere, now, missy, those belong ta us." One said in a gravelly voice.

I looked at Chance and a sinister grin shown on both our faces. Miss Zadie looked at Chance, "Must you?" She sighed, "Very well, carry on."

Chance and I began pounding the ruffians and giving them what for. We were too busy to notice that Charlee and Miss Zadie were forced to give up the tintypes at gunpoint.

We had just flattened to last one when we heard Von Duggery laugh manically as he left the store.

We looked at Charlee. She no longer had the tintypes and Whitetail came back in the back door. "He got them back? Plusterpot!" I growled.

"I'm so sorry, Dub. He had a gun and got the drop on us." Charlee was quite upset.

"There's one good thing, here." Whitetail began.

We all looked at him, "What is that?" Charlee asked.

"I've never seen those images, so I would wager no other guide has either. That means we can find them sooner than he will." Whitetail had a most intriguing grin on his face.

"How is that? He still has the tintypes." Miss Zadie asked.

"Those tintypes do belong to The Monkey Heckler and I know where to find him." Whitetail looked out the front window.

"Who is this Monkey Heckler?" I looked at Charlee.

"An old photographer. He always seems to photograph clues to the past. It's been said that he finds clues to treasure, finds the treasure and then leaves it just as it was." Charlee turned her head to look out the front window as well, "Which means he has probably already deciphered the items in the pictures."

"Whitetail, how far away is this Monkey Heckler chap?" I walked toward the window as well.

"It isn't safe to talk here. We need to leave as soon as possible." He opened the door and headed out.

"I say, why are we in such a rush?" I expressed as we all followed Whitetail.

"Shh." Miss Zadie said as we exited.

We all ran around the corner and climbed aboard The Bilious. We listened as the steam began to flow and then the fans began to turn. In a few moments we were in the air, not unnoticed however.

Von Duggery and his men were running back to the Domination as fast as ever they could. I assumed they planned to attack us. "Hurry, Charlee. We can't lead them to him." Whitetail was quite concerned.

"Where am I going?" She asked.

"The Grand Canyon; I believe he has found something there." His explanation was intriguing.

"Sorry, folks, we'll be flying through the night." Charlee looked over her shoulder.

"Charlee, we are flying north and I believe the canyon should be west of here." Chance stated.

"Chance, that cannon happy fool in the balloon is in the air. He doesn't need to know where we went." Charlee was right, of course. We made a large circle until he was out of sight and then we turned south.

As the sun settled behind the mountains, I noticed that Chance and Miss Zadie cuddled together and began to nod off, "Chance, shouldn't we stay awake and keep Charlee alert?" I whispered in a rather angry tone.

"That will be your task, old friend. I am going to get some sleep so that I can take over the controls in a few hours. You keep watch and do whatever she needs keep going." Chance smiled and turned his face into his wife's cheek.

I moved closer to Charlee, "I will watch for Von Duggery. Chance said he will take over in a few hours."

"We will be there in a few hours. We can move pretty fast in this thing, but it will be a bit cool. If you would, in the chest in the back there are blankets. Can you get one out for everyone?" Charlee smiled at me.

"I shall." I stood up and walked back to the trunk and pulled out five blankets. I walked around and handed them out to everyone. I walked back up to Charlee and wrapped a blanket around her shoulders.

"Thanks, Dub." She smiled at me again.

"I have a strange, uneasy feeling about the Grand Canyon." I sat down and wrapped the last blanket around my own shoulders.

"What do you mean?" Charlee looked at me with an honest concern in her eyes.

"I feel as though we shouldn't be going or perhaps more like a foreboding." I was never good at explaining my feelings.

"I have been there numerous times and I assure you, we are perfectly safe." I tried to smile at her words, but I was far from convinced that this was a good idea.

I watched Charlee for a few minutes. I watched how she moved the controls and The Bilious would respond, "Charlee, if I may, what are you steering to? I mean, you're not using the North Star or any other star as far as I can tell. How do you know where you are headed?"

"I came down the Continental Divide and found the Colorado River and followed it to the canyon. It's very large and may take a while to find The Monkey Heckler." She explained.

"Continental Divide?" I knew that I had studied this at some point in my life, but right now I was at a complete loss.

"The Rockies split the country. All of the rivers on one side of them flow to the Mississippi River; all of the rivers on the other side flow to the Pacific." As soon as she finished, I remembered reading the same information.

"Yes, of course." I thought for a minute, "Charlee, why are we looking for this Monkey person? Wouldn't it be easier just to take the tintypes back?"

Charlee giggled, "He's not a Monkey person. He is a very intelligent person and if he took those pictures then he has already found all the clues and might be able to help us."

"Couldn't he just tell us where the clues are and what they mean?" I thought I had the solution.

"He probably could, but he won't. He thinks everyone should be able to see things for themselves." Charlee put her hand on my face, "I have missed talking to you, Dub. No one ever made me feel so excited to just talk."

"I feel the same way. I had not realized it until we once again were around one another." I felt rather warm when she smiled at me.

Chance sat up, "Would you please, just kiss that woman and get this over with."

Charlee and I looked at Chance and then back at one another. I didn't waste a moment; I reached toward her. She put her hand up, "Whoa, big boy. That will have to be our idea, not his."

"Yes, of course. You're quite right." I looked at Chance, "Mind your own business."

Whitetail looked over the side, "There, that shack. That's him."

The Bilious started down and landed outside the tiny cabin. A moment later, an old man stuck his head out of the door. We all climbed down from the machine and walked over, "Are you the Monkey Heckler?" I asked.

"Of course." He looked at all of us, "Greeting Charlee, Whitetail and to you three as well. Come on in." He disappeared into the hovel and a light came on inside.

He was an older gentleman with a long, curly, white beard. His hair was a tangled web of straw and he was wearing a long night gown. We all walked in and were cramped to one side, "Sit down, sit down. I assume you are treasure hunters." He turned 'round after lighting the fireplace.

"Actually, we are not. We are archeologists. We are trying to find lost history." I offered.

"Charlee is with you, so I believe you. What is it that brings you here to find me?" He was very soft spoken and yet quite direct.

"Your tintypes, Mister…" Miss Zadie began.

"Oh, forgive me. I am David Wayne; you may call me David." He smiled through his beard.

"I am Zadie Chance, this is my Husband McAlister and this is Dr. Corbyn." She smiled back, but his gaze had turned to me.

"Dr, Winthrop Corbyn?" His bushy, left eyebrow went up.

"Indeed, sir, I am." I wasn't sure whether to be proud that he knew me or afraid for the same reason.

"Your cousin took wonderful pictures of the tomb in The Valley of the Kings. I am awed by your tenacious nature." He now smiled at me.

"We all had a hand in finding that piece of history. Tell me, sir, why do they call you the Monkey Heckler?" I asked quite bluntly.

His tiny round belly began to jiggle, "I was in Guyana looking for the treasure of Oliver Levasseur. I was trying to find my latitude and longitude when a pack of monkeys began to taunt me. I believe they wanted the shiny sextant. I became annoyed and began shouting back at them. How was I to know it was illegal to shout at monkeys in that town? When I returned to Colorado, everyone wanted to hear about why I was arrested. Thus, I became the Monkey Heckler." He was still chuckling to himself.

"Oliver Levasseur? The Pirate they called the buzzard?" Miss Zadie asked.

"Yes, now which tintypes did you need to ask about?" He looked back at her.

"Oh, um, the um, the wealth in the eye of the moon." She haphazardly spouted.

"You're the linguistics expert and hieroglyphologist, are you not?" He was now excited to talk to her.

"Yes, but how…" She began

"You want to know where to find these drawings and any help I can give you to get there before… someone else?" He raised his eyebrow again.

"Yes, before Von Duggery." She admitted.

"Von Duggery? He has my tintypes? I despise that gentleman, if he can be called such." He turned and walked to a trunk and reached in, "I will help you with these."

He handed photos of the tintypes and a strange parchment to Miss Zadie, "You know Von Duggery?" I asked.

"A thief is a thief wherever you run across him. He has destroyed the lives of some of those I call friends." Both eyebrows were pointed down now.

"David, these are pictures of the tintypes, but where are the real drawings at? What is the other parchment?" Miss Zadie was trying to process information as best she could.

"The originals are in The Valley of the Ancients… well close to it, but I believe I am the only one to have been there. I will give you directions. The parchment is a copy of the 'cipher' as so many call it, of The Buzzard. If you can understand it then you will find the history you seek." He looked at Miss Zadie as if looking over a pair of spectacles.

"You have deciphered this?" Now she was excited, "Scholars have been trying for two hundred years and no one has been able to."

"Of course, it's not a cipher. Think of it as hieroglyphs. The symbols don't mean numbers or letters. They mean things or ideas. In this case, the symbols mean nearly nothing." He had a grin on his face.

"Then why write them at all?" Miss Zadie was curious to learn something new.

"First off, the pirate was about to be hanged. He threw the message into the crowd. Whom did he throw it to?" David still had the smirk on his face.

Miss Zadie thought for a moment, "No one or rather anyone."

His eyes lit up, "Wrong, he threw it to the crowd; common people who, most likely could not read, thus there would be no point in designing a cipher to decipher and then read… they wouldn't have been able to, but most of them could count."

"But if it was simple, then anyone could read it." Miss Zadie pointed out.

"Exactly, that's why there are all the symbols. They make an educated man think there is more to solve that there truly is." He was getting a bit giddy.

"If it's so simple, why hasn't anyone else deciphered it yet?" Miss Zadie was hooked.

"Because it's too simple. That leads to the mindset that it can't be that easy." At this point he was almost jittery. "You will note that in nearly every line there is a unique symbol not found in the rest of the drawing. If you count the number of symbols up to and including that symbol you get numbers. If there is no unique symbol then that is a space. Add everything between spaces and what numbers do you get?" He was quite right; there were unique symbols in most lines.

Miss Zadie scoured the parchment, "I find five, eighty three, fifty eight and fifty nine. What do they mean?"

"They are the latitude and longitude of the location of his stolen loot." David's smile grew even bigger, "5° 8 minutes 3 seconds north, 58° 59 minutes 0 seconds west. That puts you in Guyana, just off a tributary of the Essequibo River, straight off a ninety degree turn in said tributary."

"How did you know north, south, east and west?" Chance asked.

"There are only two lines that end in a bracket of sorts. They happen to be the spaces between latitude and longitude and the last line. If you write north and south alphabetically, north is first, on the left and then south is second, on the right. The first bracket points left, thus north. In the same fashion east comes first, left and the west, right. The second bracket points right, thus west." He made it all sound so easy.

"How do you know where latitude stops and longitude takes over?" Charlee asked.

"There is one indention in the entire drawing, the space with the north bracket. It had to be the place to change thoughts, as it were." He explained.

"And this led you to Guyana?" Miss Zadie smiled.

"Indeed it did." He smiled back at her.

"That's why you were in Guyana where you were arrested. Did you find the treasure?" I was excited now.

"Indeed I did, and it is still there." He glanced at me.

"You left it there?" I was flummoxed by this.

"Of course. Someone else may need to experience the fun as well." He looked back at Miss Zadie.

"How does this pertain to the drawings?" She asked.

"Who were the drawings for?" He smiled even bigger.

"We have no way of knowing." Charlee added.

"We know, or at least we should. They left it for their children and their children's children. They knew that one day their relatives would be back to find what they left for them, but they didn't want just anyone to be able to see it." He looked out the tiny window.

"How could they be sure that someone else wouldn't figure it out?" Miss Zadie was ever so hyper.

David smiled bigger than ever. "They didn't draw things, they drew ideas."

Chapter 6

The Unimaginable Wealth In the Eye of the Moon

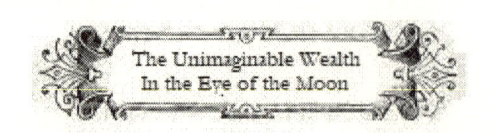

"How does one read ideas?" I asked.

"You have 'read' the drawings. They are not a sentence; they are a thought or idea. It's not 'in the eye of the moon' but rather, 'where only the moon can see'. How else would you express the idea of seeing other than a drawing of an eye?" Dave looked at Miss Zadie.

"So this one doesn't say that the wealth is bigger than everything the moon shines on. I was stumped on this one anyway. What would it be?" Miss Zadie asked.

Dave looked at me, "Vast or perhaps unimaginable. They believed that there dreams came from the moon and stars so perhaps more than one could even dream."

"The unimaginable wealth in the eye of the moon." I said.

"In the sight of the moon." He corrected and laughed.

"It also says something about the heart of the thunderbird, but there is no tintype of a thunderbird. Is there a thunderbird with the rest of these drawings?" Miss Zadie asked.

"No. Actually, you have everything from the Valley of the Ancients that you will need. Trying to hide from marauders, I guessed, they moved to what is now called the Cliff Palace. You will find the thunderbird there. I'm not going to take away anymore of your fun. Find the thunderbird and find your history. Now, off with you." He walked to the door and opened it. He stepped out and waited for us.

We all walked out. We stopped at The Bilious and turned to thank him. Charlee looked past the shack, "What was that?" She questioned and began walking quickly toward the back of the shack.

"Charlee, dear, my shack sits on an overhang. One wrong move and there is nothing below you but thousands of feet of air before you hit rocks at the bottom." David warned.

She kept walking, "I thought I saw something go behind your house."

The night was as dark as pitch and there was no moon. I panicked, "Charlee, please wait for me."

A moment later, I heard the most horrible sound of my life. Charlee screamed and I heard it fade into the darkness as if it was suddenly a million miles away, "Charlee!!!!" I shrieked and began to run to her.

David stopped me, "Stop or we'll loose you as well. I have a lamp." He ran inside and grabbed the lamp and we all ran to the edge.

There, right at the edge, was one of her revolvers and a place where the stone had recently broken away. I laid down on my belly and looked over the edge, "Charlee!!!! Are you there?" There was no reply.

David hung the lamp off the edge, but there was not enough light to see very far. Far below us I thought, for a moment I saw something move, something big, but it must have been a wisp of cloud or some such thing.

I felt my heart stop. What had just happened? I couldn't breathe; I couldn't move. I felt Miss Zadie and Chance put their hands on my back. It was at that moment that I realized that I would never see my lovely Charlee again. No one would ever call me "Dub" and I was, once again, alone. I couldn't help the pain that roared from the very center of my soul, "Noooooooooooo!!!!!!!!!!" nothing more could come from my quivering voice. One last whisper, "No, please." And I could hold back the tears no longer. I had never known such loss, such hurt. I just wanted to follow her over.

"My dear friend, I assume you are the man Charlee has told me about time and time again. She loved you more than anything, I assure you." David said to me as he brought the light back to the other side of the edge.

I slowly tried to stand. Chance put his arm around me and helped hold me up. The pain was unbearable. I had just but realized that I could love and then I was in love and now she was gone, "Come along, old friend. We should go."

We slowly walked over and sat next to The Bilious. I had no reason to go on. We sat through the night and watched as the first glimmers of light broke through the darkness. As if a million miles away, I heard a sound. I would have sworn Von Duggery was laughing at me.

I looked at Chance, "Von Duggery!"

"Yes, what about him?" Chance was confused.

"Did you not just hear him laugh?" I felt angry, now.

Chance listened, "I hear nothing, I'm sorry."

"If that man had anything to do with the loss of my dear Charlee, I will destroy him with my own two hands." I looked at Whitetail, "Can you take us to Cliff Palace?"

He nodded at me and looked at Chance, "Are you sure we should go on?" Chance asked.

"Charlee wouldn't want Von Duggery to get there first. We will give the credit for the find to Charlee, if that is acceptable to you all." I wiped the tears from my eyes. "Chance, can you fly this thing?"

"It is about the same as Shelly's so I should have no problem." He lifted my chin, "Are you well enough for this?"

I look in his eyes, "I am, old friend, I am."

"We go on then… for Charlee." Miss Zadie smiled at me and put her hand on my chest. The sun came up and shown in my eyes.

I turned to David, "Are there any other clues you can give us to ensure our successful outcome?"

"I will tell you that the symbol of the sun is also the symbol for other things as well. Oh, one other thing, pack a lunch." He smiled, hugged me and the others and disappeared into his shack.

I looked at Miss Zadie, "This will be up to you now. You will have to find the rest of the story. You two ladies are… were the heart of this endeavor and now it is on your shoulders."

Tears were still rolling down her face, "I will do my utmost to make her proud of us. I will miss her so much."

I looked at Miss Zadie's feet and there was a tiny weed. At the very top of the tallest branch was a tiny white flower. I picked the bloom and walked to the edge of the canyon. I dropped the petite bud off the edge and whispered, "I will always love you, Charlee."

I stood there a moment looking down into the canyon and then walked back, "We have history to find." I climbed into The Bilious and the others joined me. Chance took the controls and Whitetail sat up front to give directions.

The sun was warm and the air was cool. I sat at the back of the ship and looked over the side. I could remember every word she had ever said to me. I remembered ever curl in her hair, every dimple in her smile. I could still see her walking in front of me and smell the lovely scent of her hair as it swayed back and forth.

I smiled to myself and looked down at the revolver in my hand. I looked at Miss Zadie. She was looking at me. She was undoubtedly worried about my wellbeing, "Miss Zadie, I think Charlee would want you to hold on to this."

"I would be honored to. Winnie, are you going to be alright?" She put her hand on mine.

I smiled at her, "Miss Zadie, I shall never be alright again, but I will go on until the day I see her again." I looked into the clouds, "You know, just a few days ago, I was an affirmed bachelor. No woman would ever touch my soul. Look at me now, a puddle of love lost."

"You haven't lost your love. I can see it deep within your heart. Never give up on love, it will never give up on you." She smiled, "We all love you as well, Winthrop."

I looked deep into her eyes, "Thank you Zadie. I shan't forget your words." I put the revolver in her hand.

She smiled and slid it into her bag, "It's there whenever you want it."

I nodded and looked off the side once again. After a few moments, I noticed something behind us. I turned and looked. Miles behind us, there appeared a light, like a reflection off of a mirror. Miss Zadie saw me looking back. I looked at her, "Do you see that?"

The light shown across my face and she turned to look, "I do. What is it?"

I watched for a moment, "I wonder if the sun is reflecting off of something on Von Duggery's airship."

"Von Duggery?" Chance overheard our conversation, "We lost him over the mountains yesterday."

"Did we, Chance? Did we really? He may have shut down all his lights and found a way to follow us." I truly believed it was possible for him to be there,

"Whatever it is, it's reflecting the sun back at us. Surely he wouldn't be careless enough to allow something to give away his position." Chance was not convinced.

"Perhaps it is the Monkey Heckler trying to get us to return." Whitetail offered.

I squinted and looked again, "No this appears to be airborne and I don't believe he had *any* form of transportation available to him, much less an aerostat."

"Should we turn about and see what it is?" Chance began to turn the ship.

I looked at Chance. "No, I think we should get out of sight and see if it follows us."

"Right; I see the perfect place." He moved the ship a bit down and then went around a mountain which didn't reach above tree line. He quickly sat the ship down in a small clearing.

We all climbed down and pushed the ship up under the trees.

We all stood and watched the sky. It seemed like it took forever, but Bob's your uncle, Fanny's your aunt, it was most assuredly Von Duggery, "Plusterpot! How could he possibly have found us?" Miss Zadie growled.

We all looked at her without a word. She got a bit self-conscious, "What? Did I say it wrong?"

Chance started laughing, "No, my love, you said it perfectly."

"You are quite right as well, how did he find us." I pulled my revolver and stepped out into the clearing.

"Winnie, No!" Chance grabbed me and pulled me out of sight, "Let's let him get on ahead and then take off the other direction."

"That is probably wise. I just can't help but feel that he was there last night and was somehow responsible for what happened to Charlee." I glared back at the ship.

"Even if he was there, we have no evidence that he did anything to Charlee." Chance pointed out.

"I suppose you're right, but I still feel it." I could feel my eyebrows pulling together.

Suddenly the light reflected across my face, "There it is again." I looked at where it was coming from, but I was too late. The Domination floated around the next mountain and out of sight.

"What, Winnie? There's what again?" Miss Zadie asked.

"The reflection; It glanced across my face." I looked at her.

"But we are behind the ship now. How could the reflection from the front be seen back here?" She asked.

"I'm not sure. It was as if someone was trying to signal us. Perhaps there is someone we know on that ship." My eyes lit up and then sunk back, "No, I suppose that's not possible."

Chance looked at me, "We need to go now."

We pushed the ship out into the clearing and flew off toward a mountain in the opposite direction. Chance made a huge circle and came up from the south.

Whitetail looked at me, "We need to find a place to hide and sleep. We cannot go on much longer. We cannot afford to make mistakes."

"Agreed. Chance, any thoughts?" I looked at my friend.

"Indeed. I am looking at an outcropping of rock which could hide us and this ship for as long as we need. There might even be a cave behind it." He pointed down toward the ground.

"Well done ol' man. Let's head for it." I looked at Miss Zadie, "There are no beds but we do have blankets."

"I'll be fine, Winthrop. Are you going to be alright?" She smiled at me.

I looked into her eyes, "Charlee said there's always hope. So I guess there's that."

"You're so much wiser than I ever gave you credit for. I apologize for not seeing that before." She looked down.

"Heavens woman, it's your husband who is wise, I merely have the same haberdasher." I winked at her.

"I am honored to be your friend." Miss Zadie smiled.

"As I am honored to be yours." I smiled and looked at Chance, "Is there any chance we could eat something from around here?"

Chance laughed, "I will personally catch you a bush with sweet berries or find you a nice root to gnaw on."

"No roots unless there are potatoes to go along side." I snickered.

The Bilious sat down in the clearing and we all pushed it under the overhang. Chance was correct; there was indeed a cave. Miss Zadie looked around inside as we set up a camp of sorts, "No fire. Von Duggery might see the smoke." I reminded everyone.

Chance went in to find Miss Zadie and Whitetail went to find what food he could. I, on the other hand, stood in the clearing looking up into the sky. I was having a hard time convincing myself that Charlee was gone. I kept coming up with ways that Von Duggery could have taken her, but I knew that was just hope beyond reason.

Chance came running out of the cave, "Winnie! Drawings!"

I turned and looked at him. I didn't hesitate. I ran to follow him. I found him standing over Miss Zadie who was on her knees looking at rock wall, "Winthrop, it's about the thunderbird."

"What does it say, my dear?" I was excited.

"The thunderbird flew to the wall with the people." She looked quite puzzled.

"Are you reading it or finding the idea?" I was remembering what David had said.

Her eyes lit up, "Your right. The people live with the thunderbird in the wall or rather the cliff."

Whitetail stepped in with a cloth full of berries and seeds and a lantern, "What have you found?"

"Whitetail, how far are we from the Valley of the Ancients?" Chance asked.

"Not far. Maybe a mile or so. The Cliff Palace is further in the opposite direction." He explained.

"Then, this could be what they left to tell their children where they went." Chance said.

Whitetail walked closer to see the drawings. He stopped and held up the lantern. He pointed to the ceiling, "What do these mean?"

We all looked up. We hadn't seen the ones above us until the lantern arrived. Miss Zadie laid down on the wet soil and began to find ideas and thoughts. A few minutes went by, "The people are in the sky watching or seeing their dreams. I think. The sun shown through the thunderbird to give it to them?"

"Another reference to the sun through the thunderbird." Chance pointed out.

"David said that the sun could mean different things." I was a bit confused.

"Yes, but look at the drawing. The light from the sun goes in his back and then out his mouth and the dreams come from there." Miss Zadie said.

Chance took out a notebook and a pen and handed it to Miss Zadie, "Draw it and we will take it with us. Both of them."

"Excellent idea, love." She began drawing.

Suddenly it hit me, "What went into the Thunderbird?"

"The sun?" Miss Zadie was confused.

"No, no, you said it yourself. The light from the sun went in the Thunderbird." Everyone looked at me as if I were made of pudding, "Don't you see? Light goes in the bird and light comes out. That's how the moon sees it and the sun does not. Light goes into the Thunderbird and comes out where the moon can see it in the dark."

Chapter 7

The Unimaginable Wealth In the Eye of the Moon

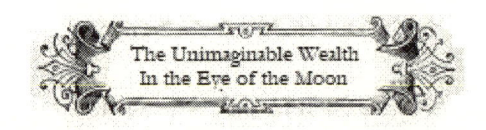

"Winthrop, you're brilliant!" Miss Zadie got up off the ground and threw her arms around me, "Chance, we have to find the Thunderbird."

Chance looked at me, "We should sleep first. Who knows what may be ahead of us."

"Oh, yes. I think I could fall asleep standing here." I haphazardly agreed with Chance.

"I am far too excited to sleep, but if you boys need your beauty sleep, far be it from me to stop you." Miss Zadie sat down and finished her drawings.

We made our way out to the exit of the cave. I noticed a very large shadow coming across the clearing. "Sshhh!" I said as I peered out from under the rock. I tip-toed back to the others, "It's Von Duggery." I whispered.

"How did they find us?" Chance also whispered.

"I think they are looking for us. As of yet, we are not found." I glanced out once again.

The Domination was almost out of sight. The flash of light ran across my face once again. I looked at Chance, "Someone saw me. That blasted light reflected across my face again."

"Are they turning 'round?" He was quite concerned.

I leaned out to look again, but the ship was gone on 'round the next mountain, "No, they are gone."

"They must not have seen you then." Chance gave a sigh of relief.

"But someone is reflecting the sun into my face. They must have seen me." I glanced out again.

"It must be a chance reflection." Miss Zadie looked at her husband, "Not you, dear."

I thought for a moment, "Perhaps they kidnapped David and he is trying to tell us, or maybe…"

Miss Zadie looked at me, "Maybe, what?"

"Charlee went back to see something that had moved. What if Von Duggery took her and flew of in the machine? What if she is the one trying to signal us?" I was excited.

"Winthrop, we all heard her fall. The airship could not have moved away fast enough that our lantern would not have lit it up even just a bit. I wish you were right, but it just can't be." Tears were in her eyes as well.

"I suppose you're right, but I will still hold to hope that it could be her." I smiled and looked around the rock.

"We need to eat and sleep. Tomorrow will be a very long day with that buzzard overhead." Whitetail placed the cloth with nuts and berries in it on a large rock.

Soon we were all bedded down on blankets and trying to drift off. I have to admit, I spent most of the night trying to think of ways that Charlee could have ended up on that airship. Most of my thoughts were preposterous. At some point in the darkness, I drifted off to sleep.

Chance woke me at first light, "Sshhh. They are right above us. They are still searching for us."

I started to get up. I was sore and stiff from sleeping on the ground. It took a bit longer than I would have liked to look out from under the rock, but as soon as I did, the light reflected across my face, "Did you see that?" I hissed at Chance.

"I did indeed. That was aimed right at you. I have been watching them since they came 'round the corner and have seen no reflection." He looked out again.

"As soon as they are out of sight, we need to get to the Cliff Palace." I needed to finish this adventure for Charlee. I couldn't help but think I was missing the obvious.

"Winthrop, we have to assume they will see us if we fly there." Miss Zadie was of earnest.

"Have you another suggestion?" I inquired.

"Whitetail, how long would it take to walk?" She looked at our guide.

"Maybe an hour and we will need to build ladders to get to the Palace." He had already begun thinking about what we would need.

"Ladders?" Miss Zadie was confused.

"Yes, to get to their homes they used ladders. There are no steps to get there, the only way is by ladder or by rope from above and even that isn't easy." He explained.

Miss Zadie looked at Chance, "Should we go ahead and fly then?"

Chance looked at Whitetail, "Which direction is the Cliff Palace?" Whitetail pointed to the right, "Excellent, Duggie went to the opposite way. We can be there before he knows we are in the air."

"Duggie is not an idiot, though he is prone to foozle effortlessly." I smiled.

"Let us proceed, then." Chance began pushing The Bilious into the clearing. We all joined in and in moments the ship was in the air.

Chance clung to the treetops so as not to be noticed. It seemed but a few minutes and we were next to the impressive, ancient domicile. Chance found a place to land and we began making a ladder from tall, skinny trees.

Whitetail would occasionally step out into a clearing and look for The Domination. "My good man, why do you do that? Von Duggery has no idea where we were headed."

He looked about once again, "I have an uneasy feeling as if we are being watched."

I said nothing, but I had the same feeling. It took a bit to make the ladders we would need to get to the cliff dwellings, but we were finally ready, "I will go up first." White tail said as he began to climb the first ladder.

"Miss Zadie, you should be next and then Chance. I shall bring up the rear and the first ladder." I was ready to explore the next finding.

Whitetail reached the top of the first ladder and reached down for the second. He placed it where he could get to the dwellings and began to climb. Miss Zadie began the first assent and Chance watched her every move.

As soon as she had reached the top, Chance followed. For just a moment, I thought I saw movement on top of the plateau. I looked again and saw nothing, "Perhaps a stag or a bear." I told myself.

Whitetail had reached the top and was assisting Miss Zadie over the edge. Chance was waiting on me, so I began my climb. As I reached the top, Chance and I pulled the first ladder up to the rock so that no one would be able to follow us.

Chance climbed up and I followed. When we reached the top I turned and looked about, "No one would be able to sneak up on you up here."

A maniacal laugh filled the valley. I knew the laugh all too well, Von Duggery! His dark, skinny figure stepped out from behind a wall, "I am fairly certain, I just did." I looked at his hand. He had a silver revolver, but it wasn't pointed at us, but rather it was aimed behind the wall he had just stepped out from behind.

"Duggie, you don't have your revolver pointed the right way. I might be able to get to you before you turn it to me. If I do, I will throw you off this cliff." I growled.

"Oh, no, Winnie, my gun is aimed quite right." He reached over and pulled someone into view. It was Charlee!

I started to run toward her, "Charlee!"

"Stop where you are or I will kill her here." Von Duggery was not one to avoid killing. There wasn't a kind bone in his body.

"If you harm her, I will remove parts of your body one at a time with a marmalade spreader and burn them while you watch." I was quite upset.

"Why loose your tongue on me? I saved her life." The smirk on his face was infuriating.

I looked at Charlee, "Are you alright?"

"Yes, I slipped off the edge and fell. I thought I was a goner, but I landed on one of the balloons of his airship and slid off onto the deck of his ship. He really did save my life; quite by accident, but he did." I had never been so happy to see anyone in my life.

"You two are pathetic. Now, where is this Thunderbird?" We all looked at him. How could he possibly know what The Monkey Heckler had said to us? He rolled his eyes, "Idiots, I followed you to the shack and listened at the door. What my little friend here saw behind the shack was me jumping onto the airship and then sinking into the canyon."

"Morley, thank you for saving Charlee's life, I am forever in your debt." I said.

"Goodness me, Winnie. You must be in love. You have never called me Morley." He hissed.

Chance began to grumble, "Chance, we can't take a chance with Charlee's life." He looked at me. He knew that at any other time, I would have jumped at a chance to attack Von Duggery.

"Don't worry about me. That's my gun he's pointin' at me." Charlee winked at me.

I remembered when she shot Duggie's ship down. She told me, "I only keep three bullets in this one." You have to turn the cylinder to get the first bullet in place. I knew I had at least three clicks of the trigger before a bullet was available.

I took a deep breath and darted at Von Duggery. Chance must have figured it out too as he followed me over. I heard the trigger click once, "Bustermott!" Duggie yelled. It clicked a second time and I grabbed the gun and yanked it out of his hand.

Chance put his mug of a fist into Duggie's jaw and we watched him fall into the adobe wall behind him, "It's Plusterpot, you maggot." Charlee threw her words at him.

"How did you get up here before we did?" I asked Charlee.

"We came down from above. His ship is above us on the plateau. His men will be down here soon if we don't do something." Charlee looked up.

I stepped to her and untied her hands. I looked in her hand and saw her silver belt buckle, "You were the one who was trying to signal me!" I said.

"I was, Dub. I'm sorry you were sad. I had no other way to tell you I was alright." She smiled.

I looked into her eyes, put my arm around her lovely waist and pulled her to me. I kissed her right there, on a cliff, in the middle of nowhere. Miss Zadie, Whitetail and Chance all cheered, quietly. I paid no attention to them. I was so happy Charlee was alive.

Von Duggery cleared his throat then humph-ed, "You're disgusting, both of you." He wiggled his jaw back and forth.

"How do we keep his men from coming down?" Miss Zadie asked.

"We don't. We do what we came to do and get out before they come down." I thought it would be that simple.

"Dub, we don't even know where the Thunderbird is." Charlee had a point.

"It has to be somewhere that it can get sunlight, right?" I was sure of that.

"Well, I'm not sure." Miss Zadie murmured. She looked at Duggie starting to crawl away, "Would someone tie him up so we don't have to worry about that wicker fuggly for a bit?"

"With pleasure!" Charlee put her boot in the middle of his back and yanked his arms behind his back and tied them together. She grabbed his collar and yanked him to his feet, "There ya go, perty as a Christmas goose."

We all had a good, quiet laugh and then started looking for the Thunderbird. Miss Zadie stopped her husband, "What are we to do with the mudsill?"

"Mudsill?" He and I said together.

"Mudsill! A disreputable person. It's a real word, gentlemen. You may look it up." She crossed her arms in defiance.

"Of course it's a real word. I use it myself. Fits this nickey bird perfectly." Charlee smiled, winked at Miss Zadie and then put the black topper onto Duggie's head, pushing it down too far. She made his ears stick out like palm branches.

"We'll have to leave him for now. We'll just try to keep an eye on him. The Thunderbird has to be somewhere the sun can reach it." Chance glanced at me and then started looking.

I understood his meaning. I walked up behind Von Duggery and drew my revolver, turned it 'round and gave him a good knock in the melon. He gave a slight, "Ow!" and then fell face first into the dusty, dirty floor.

"Winthrop!" Miss Zadie was not happy.

Charlee chuckled, "He'll be fine, Zadie. I wish I had thought of it myself." She walked over and kissed my cheek, "Let's find that drawing."

We all started looking on the outside of the adobe structure. The more we looked, the less we found. There was nothing. We all met back at Von Duggery, "There's nothing here." I stated the obvious.

"Look inside rooms and such." Miss Zadie was quite forceful.

"But, Miss Zadie…" I began to tell her something about the sun.

"Just do it, Winthrop!" She interrupted me and went into a room,

Charlee and I walked into a room with three adobe walls and a rock wall at the back. Charlee took my hand, "Dub, I'm so sorry I let Duggie catch me. You must have been upset."

"I'm just glad you're alive. I thought I was once again alone." I took her other hand, "Let's stay closer to one another from here on."

She stepped closer, "Is this close enough?"

I let go of her hands and put my arms around her. I whispered, "No." and then kissed her as I had been wishing to do for days.

A few minutes later, Charlee stepped back and opened her eyes, "I've been waiting for that for more years than I can count." She smiled and bit her bottom lip.

"As have I, but I was always too…" I looked over her shoulder. A small flash of light came through the adobe bricks in the back corner on the left side.

Charlee turned around, "What is it Dub?"

I looked at the adobe wall running from the stone wall at the back to the front of the room. I ran outside and looked around the corner. There was only four feet of adobe wall and then the face of the rock cliff going to the left.

I ran back into the room. I measured out about where the adobe ended on the outside. On the inside there was still six feet of adobe wall, "Out there, the adobe stops about here."

Charlee looked confused, "What do you mean?"

"Look, everywhere else that adobe meets stone, the adobe stops and the rock begins. Here, on the outside the adobe stops, but on the inside it continues for six or seven feet more."

"You think there's something behind this wall?" She was excited now as well, "Should we bust down the wall?"

"No, no! I saw a flash of light. There must be some way in." I walked into the corner and started looking about. There was no dirt or sand in the corner, it was stone. I looked ever so close at the adobe, "There appear to be cracks in the adobe and a chunk missing right at the edge."

Charlee walked over and helped me follow the crack. I began to blow the dust out of it. It made a complete path all the way around a chunk the size of a steamer trunk stood on end, "Do you think it pulls out?" Charlee was thinking along the same lines I was.

I leaned back, "Chance! Miss Zadie! Whitetail! In here." I yelled quietly as I could. The three came running in.

I smiled, slid three fingers into the chunk that was missing and pulled out. A piece of adobe wall about three feet wide and four feet tall swung open like a secret door in an old castle.

Chapter 8

The Unimaginable Wealth In the Eye of the Moon

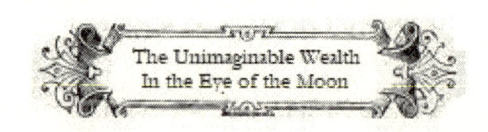

"Dub, you found a secret." Charlee hugged me.

"The passageway is lit. There is a crack in the ceiling." I pointed in and up. We all stepped inside. It was a bit of a squeeze for me because of my rather chunky frame and Chance because he was so tall, "Close the door behind us so Duggie won't follow us if his men rescue him."

Chance pulled it back into place and we began to walk down the long cleft. At the far end, the cleft had narrowed to where I could barely fit through. Just when it seemed I could fit no further, "Dr. Corbyn, there is a cave opening here." Whitetail stepped out of our sight through the stone wall.

I squeezed a bit further and slid into a very large cave. There was no light except that which came in from the ceiling. I could hear water running nearby, "We need an oil lamp or something."

Chance looked around, "Will this do?" He handed me a large stick shaped like a club of sorts. The big end was charred as if it had been used before, "It was stuck in a crack in the wall back here."

Whitetail looked at me, "The Monkey Heckler, no doubt."

"David, of course." I smelled the burnt end, "It's been soaked in lamp oil." I retrieved my trusty tin of matches. I pulled one out and struck it. The end of the club lit and the cave crackled into view.

We were standing on a very large stone, but everything in front of us was smaller chunks with a shallow spring running around them. I knew from experience that we should stay out of the water, "Don't walk in the water."

"Why?" Miss Zadie asked

"Two reasons; one, the wildlife in these caves are blind and we don't want to disturb their habitat and two, the water is so clear that you cannot truly see how deep it actually is. We should stick to the outside edge for now." I began walking around the right side of the cavern where it looked as though others had trod.

"Is this where they would get their water, do you think, Dub." Charlee asked.

"I would guess deeper in the cave where it was cooler and cleaner. That would be why there is a worn path around this side." I continued walking around the side and down into the darkness.

After about twenty minutes, I came to a place where there had been a rock slide. It had blocked the water which had made the cave that the Anasazi had built the palace in and the water had made this new course, many thousands of years ago, of course.

I looked back. Chance was having a hard time with the rocks, "Alright there my friend?"

He stopped and rested a moment, "The bullet in my leg does not care for the rocks, but I will carry on." Chance had been shot in the Sudan Wars trying to help me save our good friend, Ahmed. It imbedded itself into his thigh bone. It cannot be removed without removing most of the bone, "Perhaps I should have brought a walking stick."

I looked around and thought for a moment, "Perhaps we are ill prepared. We should go back and collect everything we will need for this journey. This must be what David meant by 'pack a lunch'."

"Has anyone seen any drawings in the rocks?" Charlee asked.

No one spoke up. Miss Zadie, also disappointed at this, looked up, "I have been looking, but I have seen nothing, least of all the Thunderbird."

"Don't you find that unusual? This was at the very least, their water supply. Why would they not put some form of markings in here?" Charlee looked all around her.

"The same reason the door is hidden, marauders." I had thought of this a bit ago.

"What do you mean, Winthrop?" Miss Zadie asked.

"If a band of evil doers or wicker fugglie were to build ladders or in some way find a way into the palace, the people would have an escape route. If there were marking on the walls, it would be perfectly obvious which way they went." I had been thinking on this very subject, "That would establish that there must be another exit."

"We will have to return to town for supplies and some rest. We can return in the morning and find the other exit." Charlee was a bit disappointed, but she knew we needed supplies.

"How do we get past Duggie and his mercenaries?" Chance pointed out.

"Hopefully he's still hogtied." Charlee smiled, "If not, we may have to shoot our way out."

I handed the torch to Chance, "You lead the way." I hoped he would feel less down on himself if he were finding the way back.

We slowly made our way back. I listened at the doorway for activity such as Von Duggery's men. I heard nothing so we all quietly snuck out into the room. Whitetail looked out at Duggie.

Whitetail looked at me and whispered, "He is still tied, but he is pretending to be unconscious. I saw his eye open."

"Then we send him on a wild goose chase." I whispered back.

We all tiptoed to the first ladder. I knew of one landmark in the American West. Wild Bill had told me about it, "Whitetail, how long will it take us to get to Devil's Tower? It could take a while to find the opening at the bottom." I whispered, but made sure that Von Duggery overheard.

"In The Bilious, a day, but we have no supplies. We should head for Denver." He played along.

We got to the bottom and loaded up. As we took off, Von Duggery's men realized that he had not returned and came down the rope ladder to get him. We were back in Salida, no doubt, before they were in the air.

We spent the night in the hotel as we had planned a few days ago and then loaded our supplies on The Bilious. In no time we were back at the Cliff Palace.

We loaded supplies into packs and raised the first ladder. I began to climb. I was almost to the top when I heard a cannon shot. I knew our ruse had not fooled Von Duggery. I had but just realized this when the ladder just above me exploded and I was flying backward toward the ground, through trees and brush. I began to climb back down as fast as ever I could, but I felt my pack hit the ground and my full body weight land atop of it. My head hit the ground and everything was black.

I felt as though I laid there for many hours trying to breathe. When I finally opened my eyes, it was nighttime. I slowly sat up. Where was I? I was no longer at the Cliff Palace, but rather on what appeared to be a vast tundra with not but rocks and very small plants.

I made my way to my feet and began to look about. There was a full moon which I knew was impossible as it was but three days since the new moon. I noticed something coming toward me. It appeared to be a person. It wasn't long before I realized that it was a man, dressed in animal skins and carrying a spear.

I noticed he had the face of a native of this land, but then it changed. The man walking toward me had a thousand faces. With each breath he took, his face changed to that of seven different individuals. He stopped and looked down at me, as he was near seven feet tall, "Bah ha nee." He spoke to me.

Somehow I knew this was a greeting, "Bah ha nee." I bowed slightly.

He looked me up and down, "Ma ooh dah?"

"I am Winthrop Corbin, at your service." Somehow I knew what he was saying.

His build reminded me of Whitetail though much taller. He had antlers of some sort on his head and what I assumed to be a bison fur wrapped around him. He seemed confused that a pale skinned man would be here, wherever here was. He looked around for anyone else, "Shah mo day bah hoo nah?"

It was very unusual speaking to a man whose face changed constantly and in a language I had never heard, but somehow understood, "I don't know why I am here, nor how I got here. I fell and awoke here." It appeared that he knew my words as well.

He placed his hand on my head and closed his eyes. I felt as though he was looking through every thought I had ever conjured in my life. He slowly opened his eyes and looked at me, "Mahnoo tah mynin imm deh minek sinto pok."

"I am him? What do you mean?" I was very confused.

A smile came across his faces, "Mec dah no zebto hok." He laughed, "Met don gek Charlee."

How he could have possibly known that I said I had no time for love, was beyond me, but then he knew how I felt about Charlee, "See here, those are private memories." I fussed at him.

He laughed louder and it seemed to thunder over the tundra, "Mon ye dok mo hoo din yah. Sin to ged ah haa da hano da lanona."

"I have always loved, but never shown it? I suppose so, yes. Not just Charlee, but Chance and his family as well. What has that to do with where I am?" I was glad he was amused, but I needed back to the others.

"Ta day mos dynonay. Tes nat ho nimno ha. Dinna boho noo ha tak. Winnie, dah hain ooh san no hah." His expression changed.

"I am chosen for what? What am I to do?" I could tell that he was of earnest.

He pointed toward the horizon on my left, "Hah doe shin shin dok zyn toe ha. Whan ooh din tek mano nah. Hey he dendo hoos tenah."

"The Thunderbird? I must find it? We are trying, you know. I understand that I must go back, but I do not know where I am now. Is the way toward the horizon?" I had more questions, but that would have to do for now.

The large figure began walking toward where he had just pointed, "Eeh tanahnee. Meh din ponee boh ha nae."

"I am the one who finds the hope of The People?" I wasn't sure I was understanding him still.

He stopped and looked down at me at his side, "Boh ha nae. Ha nae mo oh nay." He smiled and started walking.

"I, I and the ones I love?" I thought for a moment, "What of Von Duggery?"

The tall gentleman laughed, "Mo oh nay, wa hanee."

"I will love him one day too? I think not! He just shot me with a cannon!" I was furious.

He looked down at me with several stern faces, "Nok took."

"Yes, I see. It shall be as you say." I took out my chronometer and checked the time. The second hand was not moving but the minute hand was spinning wildly around the dial. The hours were passing as seconds and yet the seconds did not pass.

132

We came upon a rock. It stood fifty feet high and was a solid stone, smooth across the front. The gentleman pointed, "Mah ho nay, dok whee."

"How am I to pass through the stone? It is solid. Can I not just walk around it?" I knew what I was looking at and my body would in no way pass through a solid rock.

Again, the gentleman pointed, "Mah ho nay, dok whee." He looked down at me with several other stern faces, "Dok whee."

I looked at the rock, "Do not trust my eyes? This is impossible." I walked slowly toward the rock.

"Nok tak ben tokoey whay, chay chay la tan bin met don gek." He put his fingers over eyes.

"Close my eyes and see with my heart? How does one do that?" I closed my eyes and reached out toward the rock.

As my hand touched the rock, his voice echoed inside my head, in a thousand voices as if the world had whispered in my ear, "Find Charlee."

My hands moved around the rock. It was cold and hard and covered with dew. I moved to my left. Suddenly my left hand dropped forward as if it had fallen into a void. I opened my eyes and saw that my eyes had been deceiving me. The surface of the stone was not flat across the front.

I stepped to the side and looked around the side of the void. There was a walkway into the stone. It was four feet wide at the bottom and narrowed toward the top, but well big enough to allow me to travel inside.

I looked back at my friend, "This is the way then? Thank you so much. I do not know your name."

He put his hand on his chest, "Too woo chin." He smiled with many faces and then said, "Mah ha nee."

"Mah ha nee, Grandfather of The People." I turned and stepped into the rock walkway. I turned and took one final look at the full moon and walked into the stone.

The darkness was over powering. There was nothing I could see, I had to feel my way along the stone walls. I remembered the voices had said, "Find Charlee."

As I walked deeper into the darkness, I began to call her name, "Charlee? Charlee?" I heard no reply. I continued, "Charlee, my dear, are you there?"

I walked for what seemed to be hours calling out her name. There was nothing but darkness and silence. I was about to give up and sit down and die when I heard a faint voice, "Dub?"

I listened a bit then yelled, "Charlee, I'm here." I started running toward her voice.

Her voice was louder, "Dub! Are you alright?"

"I am here! I am coming." I ran harder. Suddenly I realized the floor was no longer under my feet. I was falling and falling and falling.

I could still hear Charlee, "Dub, Dub, don't you leave me!"

I finally hit the ground. The wind was knocked from my body once again. I could hear Charlee's voice, but I couldn't make out what she was saying. Suddenly I heard Chance, "Winnie, you plusterpot, wake up or I'll slap you silly." His hand slapped my face to the left.

The light reached my eyes and I slowly began to open them. Chance's meaty hand slapped my face to the right. I reached up and grabbed his hand, "Don't do that."

Charlee grabbed me and pulled me up, squeezing the life out of me once again, "Dub! You're alive!"

"Thanks to you. I could hear your voice and it kept me walking toward you. Without the thought of you, the last few hours would have been unbearable." I looked into her eyes.

"Hours? Dub you just hit the ground two minutes ago." She was confused.

I thought for a moment and was about to explain when Von Duggery appeared in the clearing, "Rumple wagon! You're not dead. Oh well, I'll try harder next time. Did you really think I wouldn't see right through your pathetic attempt to send me on a wild goose chase? I knew you would be right back up here."

I thought about what Too woo chin had said about Von Duggery, "Morley, what is it that you think we are going to find out here?"

"Treasure beyond imagination, of course." He bubbled.

"May I offer you a thought?" I smiled at him.

"What would that be?" He grumbled back.

"If you were an Anasazi who built these dwellings and farmed and gathered from this area, what good would gold do you?" I knew he would be unable to answer.

"Well, it would make you able to buy whatever you needed." He tried.

"There was no form of currency. There were no stores or shops. If you needed something, you built it or gave someone who could make it some food. Food was their currency. Gold would have been not but a yellow rock." Charlee helped me stand.

He thought for a bit while his men murmured amongst themselves, "You're must be wrong, because they are the ancestors of the Aztecs and their cities of gold."

I took a deep breath, as I had not been able to until this point, "Has anyone ever found a city of gold and been able to prove it?"

He smiled enormously, "I'll be the first!" And he laughed his maniacal laugh once again.

Chapter 9

The Unimaginable Wealth In the Eye of the Moon

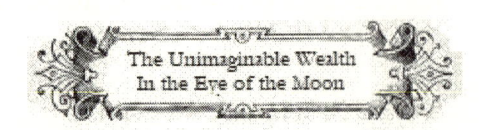

I looked at the figure of Morley. He was thin as a rail and slightly hunched. His face was beginning to look worn, just as mine was. I was quite certain that he had never known compassion, "Morley, what is the most important aspect of our quest here?"

"That I am the one to find the incredible treasure. What else?" He smiled under his oily mustache.

"What happens if you are not the one to find treasure or if perhaps the treasure is not what you think it should be?" I knew his answer, but I had to try.

His single eyebrow curled into devil horns, "Then I will have to find a way to improve my circumstances. If I don't find it then I will eliminate those who do and claim the find for myself. We have already discussed how we know the treasure is real." He turned and looked at his airship.

"What would you think if I suggested that we all pool our resources and find it together?" I knew that wouldn't go well with Chance.

"Over my dead body!" Chance snarled.

"Hear me out, old friend. We all have unique gifts to bring to the table. I think it beneficial to bring in our friend Morley, here." I gave Chance a look of "Work with me!"

"I can't imagine what *Morley* has to offer, but I'll listen." Chance grumbled.

Von Duggery slowly turned about, "You would work with me?"

"Of course, Morley. It may take all of us to figure this out." Charlee was still helping me stand, but tried to help convince Von Duggery.

Morley looked at his men who were fussing and talking among themselves, "I suppose we could help each other out, but I get credit for the find."

"No, Morley. We all do, including your men; they helped out as well." I thought perhaps I could win them over as well.

"They are not but hired help. They deserve no credit. I will join your expedition and we will share the wealth." He still had a greasy, evil look on his face.

"Now, would you be so kind as to help us rebuild the ladder which you shot with the cannon?" I tried to smile.

"No." Von Duggery thought for a moment, "Oh, very well. Men help them rebuild the ladder."

His men looked at him and then at me. Three men stepped forward and began working on a new ladder with Whitetail.

"We will need lanterns and perhaps rope." I said to Charlee as I stood on my own.

"For what? I searched that whole dwelling. There is no Thunderbird." Von Duggery growled loudly.

"Then you found the cave?" I was a bit snippy, but I had just been shot with his cannon.

"Cave?" He pondered for a moment, "That's why you were gone for so long."

"Indeed it was. We followed the cave into the rock for twenty minutes or so and then decided we needed more equipment." I gave Von Duggery a self-satisfied grin.

"I would have found it if I had known what I was looking for." He huffed at me.

"How much do you know about caves, Morley?" I was curious.

He looked at me as if I had asked his life story, "Well, geologically speaking or archeologically speaking?"

"My guess would be both." I looked into his eyes.

"I know a great deal geologically, but I must admit early native culture here in the Americas is not my forte." He was quite honest and I felt as though we had begun to speak the same language.

"I believe we came across the reason that this cliff area was inhabitable when the Anasazi found it. There had been a cave-in many, many centuries before they got here that had changed to course of the underground river." I offered a bit more information.

"You found water as well?" He asked.

"Indeed; just inside the cave." I was pleased as Von Duggery was beginning to get a bit giddy as well.

He turned to his men, "Is that ladder ready yet? I must see these things for myself."

I noticed the looks he got from the men working on the ladder, including Whitetail, "Thank you all for helping us with this."

"We are ready to ascend the cliff wall." Whitetail smiled at me, but he glared at Von Duggery.

Chance looked at me and whispered, "Are you sure you know what you're doing?"

"I believe I do. I will explain later, but I was told that Von Duggery would become one of our greatest assets. Please trust me on this." I put my hand on my dear friend's shoulder.

Von Duggery looked back at us. He looked Chance up and down and then said, "Do you still have a bullet in your leg?"

Chance looked at me and then back at Von Duggery, "I do, yes. Why do you ask?"

"I injured my knee a few years back and a gentleman in my employ pulled out some leather and metal and built me a brace which I thought might help you in the cave." He whispered to one of his men who ran toward the airship.

He soon returned carrying a long, thin item wrapped in cloth. Von Duggery took it out and handed it to Chance, "The bigger belt goes around your upper thigh and the smaller goes around your upper calf. The round hinges go on either side of your knee. It should take the pressure off your leg and make it easier for you to move along the rocky terrain."

Chance had a look of shock on his face. He took the brace and Miss Zadie helped him strap it on. He walked about in a bit of a circle and then looked at Von Duggery, "Thank you Morley. This should help out a great deal."

"It is yours now, I have no use for it anymore and it just takes up room on the ship." I don't think he liked being thanked.

I looked around at our ragtag group. Miss Zadie looked as if she was about to cry, seeing her husband able to move his leg better than he had in years. Charlee had her hand in mine and Whitetail and Von Duggery's men were chatting like old friends.

Von Duggery kept looking at Charlee and Miss Zadie as if there were something he needed to say, but he did not utter a sound. I looked at Charlee and whispered, "We will have to find Morley more friends. I don't believe he has ever been this close to a female in his life."

"He did save my life, even if it was just an accident. I owe him at least that much." She smiled at him.

"Is someone going to climb this second rate ladder or am I to be first?" He grumbled and began to climb.

"Right behind you, Morley." I started up the ladder as soon as he got to the top.

Some of Von Duggery's men stayed with the ship, but two men came with us. They were, of course armed, "Morley, wouldn't it be prudent for your men to be carrying lanterns rather than guns?" I dropped a hint.

"Perhaps, but I want to maintain the upper hand." Von Duggery still clung to his fear of not being the one to find everything, "They can carry both."

We all walked into the room where I found the door. Von Duggery looked about, "I see no cave." He paused and then growled under his breath.

I smiled at him and swung the door open, "Our next adventure begins."

"Corbyn, you magician; I am impressed." His smiled pushed his greasy mustache up onto his cheeks.

We all squeezed into the opening and lit lanterns. I walked around the side and into the cave followed closely by Von Duggery. His face lit up like a birthday cake, "Morley, welcome to Von Duggery Cavern."

"I didn't find it. Why would you name it after me?" He questioned.

Chance was a bit perplexed as well, "Yes, why?"

"This is our first true exploration of the cavern and he is our geologist. I may never have thought about a secret door if I weren't thinking of a way to hide from wicker fugglies, so this is Von Duggery Cavern." I smiled at Charlee as she stepped up next to me.

"Let's get moving." Von Duggery grumbled and began to walk into the depths of the cave.

We all started moving and after a few minutes I looked back at Chance. He was right behind me. The leg brace was working perfectly. Miss Zadie caught my eye; she was holding the lantern for Chance and her as well. I could see the tears in her eyes as she watched her husband move up and down the rocks with ease.

I couldn't help but think to myself what a wonderful gesture Von Duggery had made to a man who, only a few moments before, had been considered his enemy. Perhaps, he would be a valued member after all.

Charlee took my hand, "I'm so proud of you, Dub."

"How's that?" I looked at her for a moment then back at the uneven ground we were on.

"You took Morley under your wing, as it were. We might actually be able to trust him, thanks to you." She smiled as I helped her up onto a large rock.

I stopped and looked at Charlee, "When I hit the ground, I woke in a very strange land, a tundra and there was a man there. Well, I guess he was a man; he may have been more than man. Anyway, his face changed constantly from that of one person to that of another. He told me that Morley would be one of the people that would be considered a friend by the time this business was through. If this is indeed a possibility, then I can't let Von Duggery down."

I looked in front of us. Von Duggery was standing there looking at me, "Changing faces? A tundra? Friends? You hit your head, Corbyn." He turned about and continued his walk.

After a bit we came to the cave-in, "I think you're correct, Corbyn. This must have changed the path of the water and opened the original exit of the water to the natives who built the cliff dwellings there."

"Yes, but where do we go from here?" I asked.

"Forward, my dear Corbyn, forward." Von Duggery laughed at his own joke and began walking deeper into the cave.

Hours later, I noticed that the water was moving much slower and seemed to be rather deep, "Morley, is it just me or is the water moving slower?"

Von Duggery looked down to his left, "You are quite right, Corbyn, we just passed a natural dam. These pools could be very, very deep."

We continued on along the rock floor and eventually came upon what looked like a second branch of the cave which was a very short opening near the floor of our walkway, "Is that a way out of the cave?" Charlee asked.

Von Duggery got down on his belly and scooted his head and shoulder through. He slid the lantern through. A moment later, he slid back to us, "There is a sheer drop of some three hundred feet."

Chance kicked a rock through the opening and we all heard it fall and hit rocks a fair distance below us. He looked at me, "Definitely not going that way."

Von Duggery had gone on up the path. We heard his voice, "We are at an impasse."

We all followed him and came to a huge boulder which covered the entire walkway. There was a rock wall on one side and a bottomless pool of water on the other. The boulder reached to within six inches of the ceiling of the cavern, "What do we do now?" I was unsure of our next move.

Whitetail walked closer, "There is an Indian Ladder over here. It's right next to the cavern wall so it is invisible unless you walk next to it." He pointed out.

"What is an Indian Ladder?" Miss Zadie asked.

"Hand and foot holds cut into the rock. The stone is darkened with the oils from their skin. Yes, they climbed over the rock here." Whitetail explained.

"Climbed to where? There isn't enough space to stick your head through, much less to climb through." Von Duggery growled.

Whitetail shrugged. My lantern couldn't project to the top corner of the stone, so I put the lantern in my teeth and began to climb the ladder. I was afraid for a moment that my beard would catch fire from the heat, but it did not.

As I neared the top, I saw a crevasse, like the one at the opening to the cave, but running up, "There is a crevasse up here. I think the ladder continues up into it." I took the lantern out of my mouth to speak.

I arrived on top of the rock and indeed the ladder went on up into the opening in the rock. It ran up and to the left, toward the other side of the rock. I expected the ladder to then turn downward in such a way as to go up and over the boulder, but I was wrong. It went up into a completely different cavern. When I reached the top, I stuck my head and lantern out and looked about. The rock that I had been climbing on had separated on the back side and there was a hole forty five feet across going down at an angle so much farther than my light could reach.

I brought the light back to my side of the stone and looked down at the others climbing up, "There is a very large, bottomless hole up here…" my words were interrupted by the sound of Charlee screaming. She had missed a foot hold and was falling back down the long climb toward the boulder at the bottom.

There was nothing I could do. Chance and Zadie were between me and her. Von Duggery's men tried to grab her, but she was past them before they could grab her.

In the darkness, I could just make out Von Duggery turning sideways, finding a foothold on the other side of the crevasse and grabbing Charlee's gun belt as she neared him. He swung her into the wall and back onto the footholds.

"Charlee, are you well?" I stammered.

"Yes, I'm fine; a bit shaken, but fine, thanks to Morley." Her voice was quite shaky.

"Yes, Morley, thank you." I said with great relief.

"For what?" He grumbled.

"You saved her life. You are a hero." Miss Zadie had been quite worried as well.

Von Duggery rolled his eyes, "I must be getting soft. You people are batty."

Chance cleared his throat, "Winnie, where does this ladder lead?"

"Oh, yes, of course." I pulled the lantern back up and noticed that the ladder led to a wide ledge going across the open hole to what appeared to be another cavern, "There is a wide, rock ledge and the journey then continues."

"Might you continue, then? We are all standing on our toes waiting to move on up." He complained.

"I am sorry, old friend." I made my way to the ledge and helped the others up.

Von Duggery's men began mumbling to each other, "For heaven's sake, what are you two on about?" Morley grumbled.

One held out a lantern toward the hole, pointed to the huge stone wall dropping into oblivion and said, "Diamonds?"

We all looked over to see billions of tiny shards of what looked like cut diamond glittering back at us, "It can't be." I murmured.

Charlee looked down and found one in the rock we were standing on. She squatted down and said, "They are quartz."

Chapter 10

The Unimaginable Wealth In the Eye of the Moon

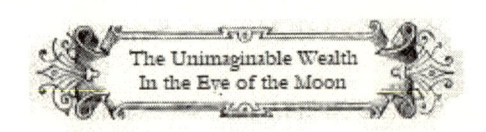

"Quartz crystals? That would explain why they appear to already seem to be cut; although, it does seem a bit strange to see them in this type of growth." Chance looked about the whole area.

"Worthless! They are not treasure." Von Duggery grumbled. He began walking toward the next cavern.

As he walked into the opening, he stopped and looked back at me. His eyes opened wide. I looked behind me, feeling very unsettled. There was nothing there other than Chance and Miss Zadie. I looked back at Von Duggery, "What is it, my good man?" I was perplexed.

"My lantern touches nothing but the floor." He almost gasped.

I moved to where he was standing and looked inside the opening, he was quite correct. The lantern lit the floor, but the walls had to be hundreds of feet away in every direction. The floor was mostly stone with a bit of sand. I walked into the emptiness holding my lantern as high as I could.

I continued to check my steps before I took them, just to be sure that there was a floor there before I tried to step on it. I stopped and looked up. I could faintly see the light from my lantern above me. It appeared to be a smooth, rock ceiling.

Then, out of the corner of my eye, far to the left and forward quite a distance, I saw a tiny flash of light. I turned my head and my lantern in that direction, but there was nothing there, "Did anyone see that?" The echo was unending.

"What did you see?" Chance asked.

"A spark or something like that. It was there and then it was gone." I put my lantern on the floor, stood in front of it and peered into the darkness.

Suddenly, I saw it again, but it was much closer. It was a greenish-yellow light and it lasted but a moment, "There, did you see it? It looked like…" I paused. Then it lit again, right in front of me, "A firefly! How could it be way down here?" It flew past my head and toward the others.

"It could have gotten down here the same way we did, you oaf." Von Duggery was not one to be kind with his words.

"Plusterpot, it would not have traveled this far without plants. Fireflies do not live in caverns. We must be close to an exit." I snipped back.

"You two stop fussing. It didn't come into this hole the same way we did, so where in this great, rock corral did it enter from?" Charlee had a wonderful way with words.

"I first saw it in the left front. Perhaps it came in from there." I picked up my lantern and began walking in that direction. I stopped looking at my steps before I took them.

As I walked the wall began to show, but the sand began to cover the floor. That's when it happened. I stepped onto sand which had no stone underneath.

My foot went down and I fell forward. My lantern flew over and landed on rock and shattered and went out. My hands found rock on the other side of the hole I had stepped in and I grabbed it. I was hanging from my elbows and one foot across a huge pit of blackness, "Heavens, I need assistance." I could not see the bottom of the crack in the floor. In point of fact, I couldn't see anything at all.

Everyone came at a slow pace while watching where they were walking. As soon as Chance and Miss Zadie arrived, they sat their lanterns down and began lifting my leg, "Good gracious, no! Don't lift my leg; I'll fall headlong into the abyss."

Von Duggery stood watching. Charlee and one of Von Duggery's men ran around the hole and grabbed my arms. The other of his men stood with one foot on either side on the hole holding the lantern up so everyone could see.

Suddenly, Von Duggery started laughing in his maniacal chortle, "Corbyn, put you silly boots on the floor. It's only four feet below your belly."

Everyone stopped what they were doing and looked into the hole. I unhooked my boot from the other side of the hole and dropped into it. I looked up at the faces staring down at me, "I couldn't see the bottom. I didn't know."

"Watch where ya put yer clod hoppers. Ya gave us all the wily-bumps." The gentleman standing over the hole said with a grumble.

"I do apologize. What is your name, by the way?" I stuck my hand out so he would help me out of the hole.

"You want to know my name?" He seemed bewildered.

"Of course, we are sharing this adventure." I assured him.

He looked at Von Duggery and then back at me, "I be Nathan Larue, sir." He took my hand and shook it.

I grabbed his hand before he let go and began to pull myself out of the hole, "An honor to know you Nathan."

"You may call me Nate." He smiled as I returned to the same level as everyone else.

"I'm Manny, Manny Prescott." The other of Von Duggery's men said aloud.

"An honor to know you as well, Manny." I looked over and then at Chance, "Do you see where the firefly came in at?"

Chance turned around and held up his lantern, "There is a dark area in the corner. I would say it is there."

"Someone else will have to lead the way. I have discombobulated my lantern." I kicked the carcass of my lantern.

Von Duggery walked to the front, "Must I do everything?"

We all started walking with Manny bringing up the rear. Chance stopped and turned about, "Where did the firefly go?"

"To fide a place to hide from Corbyn, no doubt!" Von Duggery grumbled. He stopped at the opening and listened, "I... I hear something."

We all moved to the opening. Just faintly, you could hear what sounded like pouring water, "It sounds like water being poured onto a rock." Whitetail pointed out.

Charlee listened, "It's an underground waterfall, but it's a long way away. That could be how the firefly got in; if the water is coming from outside."

"Indeed, you must be correct." I offered.

"Then where is the water going? It isn't coming here." Von Duggery hissed.

"Morley, it could be the source of the other underground stream we were following at first." Charlee reminded him, but her eyes lit up, "Look, cave drawings!"

Along one wall of the entrance to the next chamber were hundreds of drawings of people walking in the same direction. Intermingled with them were animals of varied sized and shape, "They all seem to be following the hunchbacked fellow with the flute." I was intrigued.

"That's Kokopelli. He assured that they had plenty to eat and that they had children to carry on. Did he lead them down here?" Miss Zadie was excited now.

"You mean that this fellow was their fertility god?" I asked her.

"In a way, he was the part of nature that ensured fertility." She was studying the other animals, "Why would they come down here so far and bring animals… what are these animals? Charlee, did they have domesticated animals?"

"It's possible, but we don't know for sure." Charlee was a bit perplexed as well.

Chance took a breath, "They went that way." He smiled, "I would guess we follow the sound and we will find our answers."

Miss Zadie was still looking at the drawings, "This animal is huge; how would they have gotten it up the ladder we just climbed?"

"Corbyn is huge and he climbed it. Problem solved, now let's carry on." There was nothing in Von Duggery's being that would ever make him speak less abrasively. He was just Von Duggery.

As we moved into the next chamber we found carvings all over the walls. We each moved to different places and tried to make heads or tails out of what we saw.

Charlee and I ended up looking at the same picture. A picture of what we assumed to be the sun setting, but it appeared to be landing actually on the ground with fire and flames coming out, "Is this a volcano?" Charlee asked.

"No, there is no indication of volcanic activity around here. Perhaps it was a meteorite." I really had no idea.

The next drawing had the same 'sun', but it was leaving the hole it made in the ground and Kokopelli was dancing around the hole which was filling with rainwater from the thunderbird, "It made a lake and the thunderbird filed it." Charlee noted and then moved to the next drawing, "Dub, Kokopelli brought the people to live under the lake."

I moved over and looked as well, "Under the water?" I questioned. I turned to Chance, "Chance, ol' boy, come check this drawing."

Chance looked over his shoulder, "I think you should see this first."

Charlee and I walked over to where Chance and Miss Zadie were staring up. There was quite obviously a drawing of the Cliff Palace, but standing in front of it was a monster, "Heavens, what is that?"

"That, my dear friend, would be the reason the Anasazi left the cliff. This thing was reaching in and eating them." Chance said with absolute certainty.

"It looks like a giant insect or something." I noted.

"Whatever it was, they had no weapons to deal with it." Chance looked a bit nervous.

Von Duggery cleared his throat, "It would appear that the sun shot it; the monster I mean."

We all walked over and looked at what he had found. It was a drawing of the same creature, but there was a beam of light coming from the sun and hitting it in the head, "Perhaps it died of thirst or something of that sort." I was grasping at straws.

Manny held up his lantern to see the wall in front of him, "No, it was the fellow in the sun what shot 'im."

"Fellow in the sun? What fellow in the sun?" I walked over and looked at what he saw, "There is a figure riding in the sun and I think he is waving at the people."

Everyone filed over and looked. Charlee looked at me, "The sun made the lake as well."

Chance looked at me, "Lake? What lake?"

"I was about to show you when you found the monster. Here, come look." I walked to the drawing we had seen before, but as I did I noticed one more drawing. The lake seemed to be sending water to the people below it. I stopped and looked, "Charlee, does this show the lake as the source of the underground river?"

"I think you may be right." She started to stare at the drawing.

"Winnie, the sun?" Chance asked.

"Oh, yes of course." I stepped over and pointed out the first drawing, "Here, the sun came down and made a hole in the ground."

"I would say it is the sunset." Miss Zadie offered.

"As we thought as well, but then we saw this." I showed the sun leaving and the hole remaining, "Is that not Kokopelli dancing about and the thunderbird raining into the hole?"

"How does the sun make a hole in the ground?" Miss Zadie asked.

"That may not be what happened, but this is their explanation of what did happen." Chance pointed out.

"True, but then it gets strange, Kokopelli directs the people to live under the lake." I moved to the next drawing.

"Underwater?" Chance blurted out.

"That was my question, exactly, but then I just saw this picture. They are living underground… under the lake and the lake is sending them water." I stepped next to Charlee, who was still looking at the drawing.

"Dub, they are growing food down under the lake." She almost whispered.

"How can one grow food underground? There is no light." Von Duggery snipped.

"Plusterpot, Morley, we all know that, but that is what this is saying. We merely have to decipher the idea behind it." I snipped back.

"Maybe, they are not below the lake but rather downstream from the lake." Charlee had come up with a viable answer.

"Of course. That makes perfect sense." I smiled at her.

"Then where they moved to must have been close enough to this place to allow them to come down here and draw these drawings." Chance was thinking aloud.

"Yes dear, we must be close to a way out." Miss Zadie hugged her husband.

"We should stop and eat something." I pointed out.

Von Duggery humphed, "Always worried about that stomach."

"Judging by the fact that you are as thin as a rail, I would chance to guess that wonderful food has never graced your lips." I smiled at him, "Here, try this."

Von Duggery reached out and took the item in my hand, "What is this rot?"

"The man at the general store said he called them corn dodgers. Oh, and here," I reached into my pack and handed him something else, "This is what they call a biscuit over here."

Von Duggery ate the corn dodger, "That was quite pleasant. I tasted honey in it."

"Indeed, and the biscuit is more of a form of bread over here." I nudged him to try it.

"Very light and fluffy. I like this as well. Thank you, Corbyn." He continued to eat.

"My pleasure, Morley." I smiled. I noticed Nate and Manny looking at me, "Gentlemen, there is plenty. Help yourselves." I held out the pack.

"Thank you sir!" They both ate, shall we say, vigorously.

We all sat and listened to the low splatter of water off in the distance and ate a bit of what I would assumed to be dinner. I pulled out my chronometer at looked at the time, "Heavens, it's nearly ten p.m."

"I think we should make camp here and continue our exploration in the morning." Chance was in need of resting his leg I believe.

Everyone began setting up a bed roll. Von Duggery kept looking at the drawing of the sun shooting the monster, "This means something, but what?" I over heard him talking to himself.

I walked over, "Morley, are you alright?"

I seemed to startle him a bit, ""What? Oh, yes, Corbyn." He paused, "There is something here that we are not getting. The idea, as you put it, isn't coming through. I am uncomfortable with this drawing."

"I understand your concern, but I am quite sure that the monster is long gone by now." I tried to reassure him.

"I'm not worried about the monster, you fool. It's the sun shooting it that bothers me. They had no weapons of any sort at this time, especially not ones that shoot, so what was this?" He now had me concerned.

"Are you thinking there might be an advanced tribe of natives?" I tried to gather what he was thinking.

"Possibly or perhaps Spanish intruders." He looked at me.

"You are thinking of Cortez and Eldorado?" I questioned.

He looked me straight in the eye, "Exactly, Corbyn, exactly."

Chapter 11

**The Unimaginable Wealth
In the Eye of the Moon**

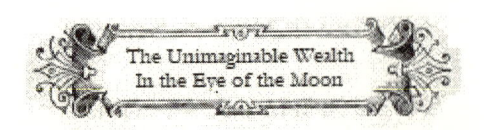

"Then explain the sun coming from the sky, making a lake and then leaving back into the sky." I huffed.

"You explain the sun having a projectile weapon powerful enough to kill something of that size." His argument was beyond my knowledge of the events.

I took a deep breath, "Morley, I have no way to prove to you that Eldorado is not here; instead, I will keep an open mind on the subject and perhaps we will both find enlightenment." I patted his shoulder and turned to go rest for the night.

He turned and watched me walk away and then he looked at Nate and Manny bedding down. He walked over to them and rather than ordering them to make his bed, as would be customary for him, he said, "May I have a bed roll as well? I am rather tired."

Nate handed him his bedroll and smiled, "Would you like me to lay it out for ya?"

Von Duggery looked him in the eye, "I am quite capable." He watched as the smile left his employee's face, "But thank you all the same." He tried to smile, but it just wasn't in him.

Nate looked at Manny and then at me. He turned back to Von Duggery, "If you need any assistance, just let me know, sir."

Von Duggery did not reply, but unrolled his bed and laid down. He closed his eyes and a moment later, we were all asleep.

I slept very hard myself. I seemed to be reliving parts of the event on the tundra I had lived earlier. The gentleman with the many faces was watching me from the rocks. It was as if he was making sure I did the things I was meant to do. In my mind, I kept hearing him say, "Whan ooh din tek mano nah. Hey he dendo hoos tenah." Which I knew meant, "You must search deep within. You must find the hope and bring the light into his heart." Find what hope and bring the light into whose heart, the Thunderbird?

I suddenly felt the being standing over me, looking down at me. I startled awake and looked up, but he was not there. Instead, the firefly was there and lit just above my head.

I slowly stood, trying to watch where he would light next. I followed him out of the room and into the next cavern. It was a smallish walkway with a smooth rock floor. I continued to follow the tiny beacon into the blackness.

As I entered the next area, I could hear the water much clearer. I thought to myself, "This cannot be a waterfall. It sounds more like hard rain on cobblestones." I looked across the area and saw the firefly go into the next section. I followed and came into another tight walkway.

For a moment, I thought I smelled something cooking; meat perhaps. I shook it off, thinking that I must be hungry. The narrow walkway seemed to go on forever. I continued to follow the firefly.

As I approached the end of the walkway, it narrowed at the top and I had to crawl. I looked toward the end where the firefly had gone and saw what looked like a small person standing between me and the firefly.

I watched as the firefly lit a few more times to be sure I had seen what I thought and I wasn't just bonkers. Each time the firefly lit, it would silhouette a small person, perhaps a child. I took a breath, "I say, are you truly there?" I was still unsure.

The firefly lit again and the figure was gone. I crawled to where it had been and looked out. There was a bit of light coming from somewhere. I looked down as the firefly lit once again. There, on the stone, next to the sand, was a small, wet footprint.

The echoes coming from behind me let me know that the others were waking and had noticed that I was gone. I began making my way through the darkness back to them. I had something to tell them that could change everything.

As I got closer, I could hear the others arguing. Charlee was quite upset, "We can't just leave him wherever he is. We have to find him!"

Von Duggery put in his two cents worth, "That hobbledehoy is so acclumsid that he couldn't walk his way 'round a quockerwidget."

I wrinkled my brow, "Hobbledehoy indeed." I took a deep breath and yelled back toward the others, "I am here. I followed the firefly."

"Stay where you are, Winthrop. We will come to you." Miss Zadie yelled back.

"It's a fair distance, but I need light." I was now disoriented from the lack of light.

It was more than an hour before they reached me. Charlee dropped to her knees and threw her arms around me, as I was still sitting on the floor. She kissed me on the cheek, "I thought we had lost you. You didn't take a lantern."

"Charlee, I saw someone." I whispered.

"You mean there are other people down here looking for artifacts?" She questioned.

"No, I think it was a child." I began, "I found a small, wet footprint where they had been standing."

"There is a lost child down here?" She was confused.

I noticed everyone was listening to us, "Charlee, what if there are still Anasazi down here?"

"You've lost you senses, Corbyn." Von Duggery snarled.

"Morley, perhaps I should beat some sense into you." I snapped back.

"Dub, how could these people survive down here in the darkness? What would they eat? Wouldn't they have to venture out into the world at some point?" Charlee was trying to use reason as she found my story unimaginable.

"Just a bit further on, there is light coming from somewhere. I assume an opening high in the mountain which has them separated from the rest of the world." I had a whole theory worked up while I had been waiting for them to arrive,

Miss Zadie looked at me, "Do you realize how impossible that would be?"

"As impossible as someone changing time to fit their own needs?" I knew she wouldn't understand, but I knew what I saw… or did I?"

I had merely seen a silhouette of what appeared to be a child. It could have been an animal and at the angle I was looking from appeared to be a human. I now doubted myself, "Perhaps I saw something else, an animal or whatnot."

"If there is one thing I have learned from being around you, my dear friend, it's that anything is possible." Chance smiled and helped me to my feet, "Now, show us what you've found." He handed me his lantern.

I turned and began walking. It seemed to take longer than it did before, but we finally came to the walkway where I had to crawl. As I reached the end, I kept checking to see if there was anyone there, but alas, nothing.

I climbed out of the far end and stood up. It was another big room with what appeared to be cavern openings all up and down and around the room. Everyone else came out and stood.

Chance looked around, "Where do we go from here?"

Von Duggery grumbled, "Maybe we should follow Corbyn's baby."

I gave him a cross look and thought to myself, "Where did the light come from?" and then, "Where did the firefly go?"

I turned and looked at Charlee, "Shut off your lanterns, everyone."

"Dub, why?" She asked.

"Trust me." I smiled and squelched my lantern.

Everyone else began to do the same. We all stood there in the pitch black world waiting for our eyes to adjust. The sound of the splattering water was much louder now.

Then, I saw the firefly. It was in front of a cavern entrance which seemed to have just a bit of light deep inside, "There! The light is there! I'll keep my eye on the opening, someone light a lantern." I found myself giddy.

Lanterns began to come on and I led everyone down to the opening. The ground was rocky and easily stumbled upon. As we neared the opening, the sound of the water was deafening. It sounded like the echo of an unending thunderstorm.

I stopped at the entrance and held up my lantern. At the top of the entrance was the drawing of a thunderbird… a very large drawing. The opening seemed to go right through center of the bird. I looked at Miss Zadie, "Through the heart of the thunderbird?"

"You found it, Winthrop." She was excited.

"Well, Corbyn, what's in there?" Von Duggery fussed.

I walked in through the opening and found myself at the edge of a bottomless pit, "Everyone stop! It's a sheer drop-off." I yelled back to stop the others. I looked around and saw a walkway going to my right and down.

At the bottom of the walkway was daylight being obscured by what appeared to be water… perhaps a waterfall. I stuck my head back out and told the others, "As you step in, turn to the right and step away from the opening for the next person. There is daylight at the end of the walkway."

Von Duggery pushed me aside and walked out into the area. He started down the walkway as if he were about to find the prize. The rest of us followed. Von Duggery had stopped in the opening. He was starring out through a waterfall, "Morley? What is it?" I asked as we all walked up behind him.

"I… I…" was all that came from him. He stood looking out as something, but what, I could not see. The waterfall was very much like rain pouring down; the true "heart of the Thunderbird" it then hit the rock and ran off somewhere.

"Morley, you must step through the waterfall." I tried to coax him.

Without a word, he took off his weapons and his pack and laid them aside on the walkway. He shut off his lantern and stepped through the water. That's when I realized that he had been starring at someone, not something.

There was a young lady standing in a field of crops not far away and they had their eyes lock on one another, "Chance, there are people here."

We all followed suit and left our belongings in the cave and stepped through the water. We were not outside, but rather in a massive hole at least a mile across. The sun was overhead and yet it wasn't exactly the sun. It shimmered as if it was in a bowl of water.

Chance looked up, "Winnie, Look at that!"

I looked at the ceiling. It was some form of crystal in the shape of a great, glass bowl. There was a river or lake on top and a thriving community below it. There were buildings and farms and trees and animals and people.

As I stood looking about, I heard Von Duggery say, "I am Morley." He had a smile on his face I had never seen before.

The young lady smiled back and said, "Ta tah nee. Mo hay Ta tah nee."

"She said her name is Ta-ta-nee." I informed Morley. Everyone looked at me.

Ta-ta-nee spoke again, "Da han no pay, Mor ley."

Everyone looked at me including Von Duggery, "She said that she knows you, Morley."

"How does she know me?" He asked over his shoulder.

"I think she means that she sees you, the real you, your heart." I turned my eyes to her, "Ot ma tino don ho nay?"

Ta-ta-nee looked at me, "Monahee shon day hee. Ponay ta dine-ay."

"She has seen your coming in dreams and is glad they were real." I said.

Whitetail looked at me, "How is it that you know these words and I do not?"

"I am not sure. I could understand the other gentleman, or whatever he was, as well, but the words did not come to me to speak back." I tried to explain, but it did not come out in an intelligible sentence.

Miss Zadie took a breath as if she had just understood everything, "This is it!" we all looked at her with confusion, "Don't you see? The sun through the heart of the thunderbird, water or rain is the heart of the thunderbird. Only in the eye of the moon; during the day, this looks like the bottom of the lake, but at night the moon can see their lights or fires. This is the unimaginable wealth. They have everything they need and no one knows they are here. These people are the Anasazi."

Ta-ta-nee, put her hands on Morley's chest, "Na to hawnee! Da nee po not un."

Morley looked at me, "What was that?"

"She said we must leave. They will end our days… I think." No sooner had the words came from my mouth than Ta-ta-nee ran out of the field and men came yelling and carrying torches and spears.

I put my hands in the air and yelled, "Bah ha nee." I bowed a bit, "Ma ho na Corbyn."

The men attacking stopped and looked at me. One walked to me, "Oha, den denay ud nah ree."

I knew he was asking why we were here. I smiled, "I have come to give you hope, May ho tin don tah wo nee hay."

"Moha dee tin no. Shee shay ta hoe en ock nah. Wo nee hay, dot nah." Was his reply.

"What did he say?" Chance asked.

"Something to the effect of, 'We have all we need. The Mother is good to us. Hope for what?'." I looked back at the Anasazi gentleman, "Toe tay sha see do har tee hoe." I looked at Chance, "I told him I was here to reunite the twelve."

"Twelve what?" Everyone asked at once.

"Haven't the foggiest. It just popped into my head." I looked back at the Anasazi. They motioned for us to follow them. One ran on ahead, "We are to follow our new friends."

We all walked out of the field and into a nearby adobe building. There sat an elderly gentleman on a hand woven rug, "Bah ha nee." I said as he looked at me.

He took a deep breath, "Mahoo day see do har tee hoe, Corbyn. Mak hee doo nah."

"Translate for us Winthrop." Miss Zadie asked.

"He wants to know how I will reunite the twelve." I explained, "I will tell him I was told to come by the man with many faces." I looked back at the chief, "Dah nee pohoh das ka too been ah. Shaa tee nah."

His eyes widened, "Ko ko pelli tah hay nee hoe da … Ah pa shay, Ho pay, Nah vay ho, Pah bah lo, Zoo nah, Ooh tay, Azah tay, Enca, Mo hah vay, Pea mah d'na Yoo mahan sha day Anasazi?"

"I think I caught all of those." Charlee bubbled up, "Apache, Hopi, Navajo, Pueblo, Zuni, Ute, Aztec, Inca, Mojave, Pima and Yuman." She repeated. My mind was stuck on the fact that he said Kokopelli had sent me.

The old man looked at her, "Hatay, mo hantee toh chay?"

I looked at her, "He asked if you know all of these people?"

"They are all tribes of natives in the Southwest and South America." Charlee smiled.

I looked at Whitetail, "Are you not Ute?"

"Yes, I am." He replied.

I looked at the old man, "Da tee hanee too bah. Hee nah day Ooh tay." I pointed at Whitetail.

The old man stood and walked to Whitetail and put his hands on his shoulders, "Bah ha nee, mah tah tee no." He pressed his cheek on Whitetail's cheek.

Whitetail looked at me. I smiled, "He said, 'Welcome, my brother.'"

"Tell him I am pleased to meet him." Whitetail smiled.

"Whitetail, mah tah tee, mohoe tan yee." I translated.

"Ma dee nah, hah teen yam tok bee hon." The old man walked back over and sat down.

"He said you should bring all of your people here, there must be so many by now." I looked at Charlee, "He has no idea what has happened outside this underground world."

"He thinks they are all still near here. They must be parts of the Anasazi that left or didn't come down here at all." Charlee was concerned, "He doesn't know about the genocide the Europeans played out against his people."

Morley sniveled, "Yes, and if he finds out, none of us will leave here alive."

Chapter 12

The Unimaginable Wealth In the Eye of the Moon

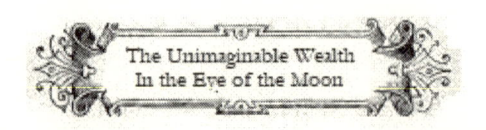

I began to think about the tundra I had been on. The old man just called the person of many faces, Kokopelli. I think I understood that at any rate. The man of many faces said I was chosen. He said I would find the hope of the People.

I don't even know if that truly happened, although I did somehow learn this language. The old man looked into my eyes, "Mohee benah tuk hay. Pah took din oray sint."

"Why am I troubled? My eyes are searching?" I was unsure of his meaning, "Maynee ent soo nee?" I asked what he meant.

"Ko ko pelli das mon hee hay tok tah doe." He smiled at me.

"What did he say, Dub?" Charlee asked.

"Kokopelli sent me here. They sent us all." I stopped and thought, "He refers to Kokopelli as a collective; a 'they', such as God is said to be the Father, the Son and the Holy Spirit. He also said not to worry."

"What are you worrying about?" Chance asked.

I looked at him, "If the persons I saw on the tundra were in fact Kokopelli, then, they sent us here to find the hope of the people not to bring hope to the people. What does that mean? Is this place not the last hope for them? Why would a god of sorts send us to find this place?"

The old man spoke, "Yatahay, Ko ko pelli. Han ta me yah tok, Corbyn."

I turned to him slowly, "I do not know the first word he said, but the rest was, 'Kokopelli is with you now, Corbyn."

Whitetail cleared his throat, "No, Dr. Corbyn. The first thing he said was 'Yatahay, Ko ko pelli.' Which is Navajo for 'Hello, Kokopelli."

Everyone looked around me. I, myself, even looked behind me. The old man laughed, "Ko ko pelli me yah dee tac nee."

"He is within me?" I was a bit apprehensive, "Moho tuc hay nee decot oh nee hay." I told him we were sent to *find* the hope of the People.

The old man's face changed. He began to look concerned as well, "Moho neb tin ock?" I shook my head. "Tah nee yockto ben yah tas hay ben yowah!" He looked over my shoulder and yelled, "Tok mohah dinay!"

The men with spears came back in and surrounded us, pointing their spears at us, "Tok tok!" They growled.

"Winnie, what did you say to him?" Chance grumbled.

"I merely told him we were sent to *find* the hope of the People. He reacted poorly and asked if I was sure we were not to give hope and then said we were never to leave here." I began walking in the direction that the spears were sending me.

"Your lack of tact has doomed us yet again, Winnie." Chance fussed.

"Lack of… now see here, ol' man. You try speaking a language you don't know and use the proper tact. I think he's just being unreasonable." I countered.

"Winnie, you do this all the time. Every time you…" Chance began.

"If the two of you don't end this bickering, they will run us through just to shut you up." Morley had listened long enough. I noticed him looking about. I assumed he was looking for Ta-ta-nee.

They led us to a sort of cage made from branches and rope. They pushed us all in and closed the door. They wove a vine all the way around the door to seal us in and the two of them stood guard.

I noticed that the sun wasn't shining through the water as much and I guessed that night would be coming soon, "Miss Zadie, how is this place the unimaginable wealth we came to find?"

She looked around, "If you had been attacked by marauders for hundreds of years and your food and belongings stolen over and over again, a place like this would be priceless, would it not?"

"I can understand that. So, only the moon can see it and daylight through the heart of the thunderbird also refer to this wonder. How is it so much warmer that the rest of the underground?" I questioned.

"It must be the sun through the water and the crystal bottom. It must warm the area down here. I wonder what happens when the water freezes over." Miss Zadie was thinking aloud.

"It is always fifty six degrees under ground, even if the water above it is frozen." Chance smiled at her.

"I would assume it would just be part of they crop's growing cycle. Their winter, if you will." She smiled back.

Morley rolled his eyes, "You people disgust me. Ta-ta-nee said they were going to kill us. The old wrinkle-bucket back there said we were never to leave; are none of you concerned with this?"

"Heavens, Morley is correct. We do need to plan our escape." I began looking at the cage.

"Get a hold on yourselves. We will find a way out without trouble. The light will be gone soon and they will not be able to see me cut the back out of the cage with my pocket knife." Chance smiled at me.

"Bully, ol' man, bully." I knew my friend would find a way.

The night grew a bit darker and two men walked over with torches and placed them on either side of the cage. Morley looked at Chance, "So much for your plan."

As the night got darker Chance looked around and decided to try to cut rope without alerting the guards. He began to cut through a rope, "You all keep your eyes on those two."

"Chance." I whispered.

"Not now Winnie." He continued to cut, "These ropes are made of leather!" He complained.

"Chance!" I did my best to alert my friend, but suddenly there was a spear stuck at his throat, "One of the guards is coming."

"Mon hee donay!" The guard growled at Chance, but then he dropped the spear and fell to the ground. I looked at Chance and he looked at me and we both shrugged.

I looked at the other guard just as a tiny arrow of sorts stuck him in the shoulder and his eyes rolled and he fell as well, "Chance, look!" It was Ta-ta-nee. She had some sort of reed and had sent blow darts into our guards and sent them to the ground.

"Tay me non meha." She looked at me and then smiled at Morley.

"She said to hurry, they will wake soon." I looked at Morley. He looked like he had found pure gold, "Morley, help me unwind this vine."

He smiled at Ta-ta-nee and began unwrapping from the other end. She bent down to help him. They continued to look at one another. I knew the looks; they were the same looks Charlee and I had been giving one another since I got off the airship.

As soon as the door was open, Morley grabbed Ta-ta-nee and hugged her as if he had been away and was just returning home. She then grabbed his hand and began leading us to the waterfall.

As we walked through the opening, we all grabbed our weapons and packs, lit our lanterns and then followed Ta-ta-nee back the way we came. We walked for hours into the darkness, "We will be getting close to daylight soon, I would guess." Charlee smiled at me, "They will be finding the guards unconscious, but we have a pretty good lead on them."

As we came upon the room with all the drawings, Ta-ta-nee stopped and walked to the walls as if she had never seen the drawings before, "Ta chee nom panose denee?" She looked at me pointing the monster being shot by the sun."

"What did she say, Dub?" Charlee could see the confusion on her face.

"She asked why the mountain is attacking her village." I looked at the drawing, "What we thought was a monster was in point of fact the very mountain we were inside."

"How does the mountain attack a village?" Morley stepped up behind Ta-ta-nee and put his hands on her shoulders.

"Yes and how is this her village? I thought it to be the Cliff Palace." I was confused.

"She has never seen the outside. Her world has been in the ground for centuries." Charlee reminded us.

Out of the corner of my eye, I noticed someone standing in the doorway we needed to travel through next. I turned my head to look, but there was no one there. I swear it was Kokopelli, but he was not there long enough for me to see, much less show him to the others.

Ta-ta-nee saw me turn my head quickly. She looked at me, "Mo hodi nee she bo nay. Mo kee Ko ko pelli?"

"I saw it too? I witnessed Kokopelli? How could she have possibly known that?" I said aloud.

"What did you see? Charlee took my hand.

"I thought I saw Kokopelli standing in the opening, but when I turned to look there was nothing. She must have seen the same thing I did." I looked at Ta-ta-nee, "Dah day Ko ko pelli me kwayho?"

She smiled and looked at Charlee holding my hand. She looked up at Morley and slid her fingers among his. It was a bit awkward as neither of them had ever done such a thing before. She looked back at me, "Ko ko pelli din nah."

"Kokopelli helps us." I smiled at Charlee.

We walked into the next room and we all watched our step after my fall over the four foot crevasse. Morley and Ta-ta-nee walked holding one another's hand. It was quite quaint to see the grumbling Morley with a smile on his face that wasn't evil.

Charlee and I watched as the two enjoyed their time together. I looked at Charlee, "If I asked you to marry me, what would you say?"

"Well. I guess you'll just have to ask to find out." She squeezed my hand and smiled.

"I hardly think this the place and time for that conversation, Winnie." Chance was not a romantic in the slightest.

"Oh, yes, quite so… I guess." I squeezed Charlee's hand back and we walked on.

As Von Duggery and Ta-ta-nee walked out onto the walkway on the edge of the abyss, he stopped and squatted down to pick up a quartz crystal to give to Ta-ta-nee, but Nate did not see him bend down and tripped over Morley, falling full force into the arm of Ta-ta-nee. She came loose from Morley's hand and fell over the edge of the walkway, "No, Ta-ta-nee!"

Morley threw Nate off and ran to the edge. We all came running to see what had happened.

Nate said, "I tripped over Von Duggery and knocked the lovely lady over the cliff. I didn' mean to. It just 'appened."

I watched as Morley turned around, squatted and then dropped off the side of the cliff, "Morley!"

I ran to the edge and held out a lantern. Both Morley and Ta-ta-nee were hanging by their fingers from a tiny ledge. "What are you doing man?"

He moved his fingers until he could get his knee under her and then helped her get her feet up on the ledge where we could reach her.

We pulled her up and I reached down for Morley, "You'll have to lift yourself to the ledge as well, Morley."

"I cannot, you oaf." Morley growled.

I looked at Charlee, "If we latch our gun belts together we should be able to pull him up."

As I stood up Ta-ta-nee laid on her belly and looked down at Morley. She reached down with both hands and tears began trickling down her face.

I could hear Morley saying something, but I couldn't make out what it was, "What did you say Morley? We are working as fast as we can."

"I said to tell Ta-ta-nee that I love her!" He yelled.

I looked at Charlee, "That doesn't sound good."

"Dagnabbit, Corbyn, tell her!" His voice was a bit elevated and echoed through the cavern.

I looked at the lovely Ta-ta-nee, her face wet with tears, "Morley, I'm pretty sure she knows and I feel she reciprocates your feelings."

We were having trouble getting the belts to buckle to one another and fussing at the leather worker who had made them different widths. All of the revolvers were on the ground in a pile as they did not seem important at this time.

"Corbyn you clod. Tell me how to tell her that I love her!" Morley was a bit upset.

I looked at Ta-ta-nee. She looked at me to see what he had said. I stopped what I was doing and walked to the edge and looked down at him, "Hah pay nay."

I walked back to Charlee and the others. Morley looked up at this woman he had seen for the first time only a few hour ago, smiled and said, "Hah pay nay, Ta-ta-nee."

She smiled at him, "Hah pay nay, Morley."

I looked at Ta-ta-nee and I knew at once that Morley Von Duggery had let go of his grip and slid into the blackness. I had started out this adventure despising that man and had come to call the grumpy wicker fuggly my friend.

Ta-ta-nee lay on the ground weeping. Whitetail walked over and laid a blanket on her. He squatted down and put his hand on her back. We all gathered around and put our hands on her back.

It was a show of support, but it was to be short lived as five men with spears stepped in and surrounded us. Our guns were six feet away and we had no recourse other than to make the long trip back to the village.

One of the original guards growled, "Ta nay be potuck?" which meant "Where is the weasel?"

To which Ta-ta-nee replied, "Potuck cha nee bem mo hay." Which was "The weasel gave his life to save mine." The guards looked at one another and then began poking us to begin walking back.

As we walked along, Charlee and I tried to comfort Ta-ta-nee. She was hurting and was still putting forth large amounts of tears without so much as a whimper.

Charlee looked at me and smiled, "They would have been so happy together."

"I have never seen Morley smile as he did when he looked at her." I agreed.

"At least they were able to tell one another how they felt, thanks to you." Charlee took my hand once again.

Ta-ta-nee saw Charlee take my hand and reached over and took Charlee's other hand and leaned against her. She began to weep again.

The guard who had asked where Morley was walked over to her, "Ta-ta-nee, mo dee mak dah nee?"

She put her free hand on his face, "Hah payn, Morley." Which was "I loved Morley."

The guard stopped her and hugged her tight. Charlee and I looked at one another. The guard looked into her eyes, "Hah tee nach, bey ood."

"What did he say?" Charlee asked me.

"I am sorry, little one." I translated.

Ta-ta-nee again put her hands on his face and said, "Hah jaw boh nee, dah rohoo."

My jaw must have dropped open, because Charlee was desperate to know what she had answered, "What, Dub, what?"

"He's her brother, older brother, I would guess." I was still taken aback.

He looked at me and said, "Hah tee nach dah nee wan."

I bowed slightly and smiled.

"Dang it Dub, what was that?" Charlee questioned.

I look at her, "He said he was sorry that he died."

We all started walking again and we were soon walking through the waterfall.

Chapter 13

The Unimaginable Wealth In the Eye of the Moon

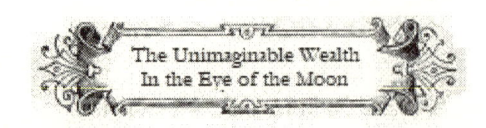

I looked around at all the people looking at us. They all seemed to be very concerned. I looked up at the morning which should have been well on, but it was dark and dreary. The waterfall was growing in volume everyone looked to be worried.

I leaned back to Chance, "Is there a storm coming over the mountain?"

"Of course there's a storm going on and these people are worried to death." He barked back at me.

I looked about again, "What are they afraid of. They are underground. The storm can't get to them?"

"I'm not sure, but they are frightened beyond explanation." He was looking around at all the faces looking up as well,

Ta-ta-nee was looking up as well. She was frightened, "Mock too nah hanee! Shin so bah hah."

"The story is happening? We brought him? What do you mean... I mean, do hah nee tock?" I translated and requested in one sentence.

"Dah hay tee poklay mo hoo. Oow chay ta kopal. Mehoshay ten hay be tashay bok no hee. Haheetonay shish do nay dehay." She looked ever so frightened.

"What was that?" Chance asked.

"She said the mountain is coming as was told to them. They are to be wiped out, but someone was sent to find them hope," I looked at Chance, "It's us. We are here to save them."

Chance looked 'round and then back at me, "First off, they are waiting to kill us. Why should we do to anything to help them? Second, she said a mountain is coming for them. How is that even possible? And third, how do we save them from a mountain?"

I became a bit cross, "Morley loved this woman. I'm not going to let her down. Perhaps the water is going to rush through here in a bit and wipe them out or there is about to be an earthquake, I don't know, but we will be here to help whatever happens."

"I do see your point, ol' chum. I agree with you. I'm not sure what is to happen, but we will solve it together." Chance pulled his wife close and kissed her on the forehead.

There was obviously a huge storm going on outside. There was lightning and muffled rumbles of thunder. The old man from yesterday met us in the center of town, "Tahawnee mo hay do nock." He was speaking to me before we even got together.

Charlee squeezed my hand, "He is very upset and not at us this time. What is going on?"

"He said we have to save them. He is coming." I explained.

"Who is coming?" She was a bit nervous now as well.

"I don't know; perhaps the monster from the cave drawing." I wasn't sure at all.

"Doesn't the sun destroy it?" She looked up.

I looked up as well. The water was becoming murky with the rain water washing mud and debris into the lake. The sun was still visible, but it was covered with storm clouds.

"Chance, you are an engineer; what would happen if too much water came into the lake?" I was concerned.

"I assume nothing. The water runs out as soon as it runs in, thus the waterfall is a bit bigger, but even the waterfall could not get big enough to flood this place because the water immediately runs out through the rocks and out into the caverns below. The only way I could see the mountain harming these people is if there was an earthquake and the bottom of the lake broke." Chance loved engineering question.

Suddenly the sky lit up like the sun had sat in the lake and then it was followed by the sound of a thousand sticks of dynamite going off all at once. The Anasazi people all screamed, put their hands over their ears and dropped to the ground as if to pray.

That sound was followed by the rumble of the ground. Everything was shaking, "Is it an earthquake?" Whitetail asked.

"I don't know what it is, but I feel it is headed right for us." Chance was looking at the old man, who was on his knees with his hands outstretched to the sky.

The rumbling got louder and louder and then things began to hit the water above us. I looked once again to Chance, "What is that?" I had to yell because the sound was so loud.

"Haven't you figured it out, Winnie? It's an avalanche!" We looked up at the mountainside rolling into the lake.

The waterfall became a rush of muddy water and then was gone. The people screamed once again and then everyone was running to us, "Dome tak nehay." They all yelled.

"What are they saying?" Charlee asked as the rumble died down.

"They are asking us to save them." I looked back at the waterfall which was now nonexistent, "They now have no water for themselves nor their plants and animals."

The storm seemed to be dying down outside, but the sun was blocked by all the stone and dirt which had filled the lake on the downhill side.

"Chance is the stone going to break the bowl of the lake?" I asked.

"I don't think it will. It doesn't weigh much more than the water that it replaced. I can't imagine how we would remove it all to save these people. I'm afraid they will have to move back out of the caverns." He said.

"Chance, you can't be serious. These people would be wiped out just as the other tribes were. They have no way to defend themselves. We have to remove the rock from the lake." I was quite concerned.

"Get off your white horse, Winnie. We don't have the resources to make this happen. I don't know what Duggie had on his ship, but his men have probably taken it back to England by now anyway. We are on our own." Chance was a bit of a pessimist.

Nate and Manny both took offence to the words of Chance, "Now see 'ere, Mr. Chance. We may not be the most educated lot, but we ain't never abandoned no one. We are all good men... well most o' us and Mr. Von Duggery was fair with us. I don't think speakin' ill of any of us is fair when you don't but know two of us." Nate was wiser than I thought.

Chance looked at the two dusty, dirty gentlemen, "I do apologize. You are quite correct, I had no right to speak ill of any of you nor of your character. If you two are any sibilance of the rest of the men, then Morley had a fine crew."

"Thank you, sir." Manny smiled.

Suddenly, people started screaming and hiding their heads with their hands. We all began looking around, "Plusterpot, now what?" I grumbled.

Ta-ta-nee looked up and shrieked, "Tawnah mohay sahsay da Morley!"

"What was that? What do you mean the spirit of Morley?" I looked up at the same place she was looking. Sure enough there was Morley floating above us, pail and skinny, "Well, I'll be a magpie's miracle!"

Morley wasn't a ghost; he was in the murky water wearing not but his skivvies, (which is why he was so white, his skin had never seen the sun) a pair of goggles and a hose of some sort in his mouth. He swam to the crystal bottom and waved down to us and then looked about to see what needed to be fixed.

He realized that the waterfall was completely plugged. He pressed his goggles against the bottom of the lake and looked at me. He made hand signals of some sort and then started to swim up, but then stopped and looked through the glass again. He looked right at Ta-ta-nee and then pressed his hand against the crystal globe.

She smiled, tears running down her face and held her hand toward him. He smiled under his breathing hose and started to back away, but something caught his eye. He looked through the bowl again, shook his head and looked again.

I surmised he was looking behind us and up. I turned around and looked up. I quickly saw Kokopelli standing on a ledge on the side of the rock wall around the village, "Kokopelli!" I said aloud.

Everyone turned around and looked. "Where? I see no one." Chance looked right where I was looking.

"You don't see the chap standing on that ledge?" I was a bit perturbed.

"No, what ledge. I see nothing." Charlee added.

Ta-ta-nee put her hands over her mouth, "Doo nee Ko ko pelli."

"She sees him… them, how do you not?" I grumbled.

"She saw them in the cavern as well, didn't she?" Miss Zadie was quite correct.

"Yes, but Morley didn't, yet he does now." I looked back at Morley, but he was not there, "Where did he go?"

Everyone turned around to see the empty, murky water, "Perhaps he went for help." Charlee was always an optimist.

"Where would he find help way out here?" I was not so optimistic.

Nate cleared his throat, "If I may, sir, there is a great deal of minin' equipment on the Domination. Perhaps, 'e went ta get some of i'. The rest of the crew would be near enough to 'elp I would say."

"Nate, you're brilliant. That must be his plan as well." I was giddy.

The storm was apparently over and the water began to clear just a bit. After a bit, some of the people began to point up at the sun. Chance and I looked to see what was happening.

The Domination was floating in the sky right in front of the sun. It looked like the airship was the sun and the hoses coming off the ship looked like beams of light hitting the rocks in the water, "Chance, are you seeing this?"

"Indeed, it's the drawing in the cavern. The Domination is the sun shooting the monster in the lake." He had begun to believe that the drawings meant something.

Suddenly it struck me, Kokopelli! I turned to where we had seen them. They were not there. I couldn't help but wonder where they were and why they had been watching us.

I turned back around and looked at the lake. There were lots of men in the water with hoses on their mouth, picking up rocks and carrying them out of the lake, "This shouldn't take too long, unless..." I began, but some of the underwater rock shifted and a huge boulder slid its way to the bottom, "Unless they encounter excessively large stones."

"Plusterpot! Winnie, how are they to remove a stone that large?" Chance was obviously upset.

"I don't know. I hope Morley has a plan. I wish we could get outside and help." I thought for a moment. The old man was still sitting on the ground nearby looking at the lake and all that was going on.

He looked at me, "Tok day noh sin shich tooway."

"He thinks we are the people of the Thunderbird." I smiled at Charlee and then turned back to the old man, "Noh sin shich tooway sot bo wee non de hay." I smiled at him, "Mee hoh tak bunay chet bahoy non non."

"Translate please." Whitetail insisted.

"I told him we were from much farther away than the people of the Thunderbird and I asked him if there was a way to get outside from here." I explained.

The old man slowly stood, motioned for me to follow. I walked with him toward the waterfall. He stopped at the edge of where the waterfall came out and fell to the rocks. He pointed up, "Natch pod deen notto pah den henah."

I looked at Chance, "He said you can walk through the waterfall into the sun. I believe the rocks are still blocking the opening at this point though."

"We will have to wait for Morley to dig it out. How do we reach it from the ground?" He asked.

I looked at the old man, "Kag nan pas day nohar."

He pointed to the cage we had been locked in, "Tan tah day."

I looked at Chance and laughed, "We push the cage over here and climb on top."

Water began to drip from the opening; a little came down and then a bit more. Before too long, water was rushing back into the village.

"Are we ready to do this?" I looked at the people around me.

"I'm coming too." Charlee smiled at me.

"I wouldn't have it any other way." I smiled back, "Let's get the cage over there." We heaved and lifted the cage. We carried it to the falling water.

Chance began to climb, "My friend, there is rushing water and no ladder up there, perhaps you should wait until we return the other direction."

He lowered his head, "I understand. You're most likely right." He stepped back down off the cage.

Nate stepped over, "Manny and I are at your service."

"Excellent, Nate." I looked up and saw Whitetail already going into the falling water, "Charlee, we should follow quickly."

The rest of us began to climb. When we reached the crevasse, I looked into Charlee's eyes, "Hold your breath and climb. Don't stop until there is nothing above you. I will help any way I can."

"I can do this, but if I stop, push my fanny on up." She smiled at me.

"Indeed I will." She touched my face and then began to climb into the rush.

I followed as soon as I could as did Nate and Manny. The climb wasn't long, but it was a bit difficult through the water. The water was icy cold and quite the bite on one's skin.

I could tell it was getting lighter as I reached the top. I reached up for the next grip and suddenly two pair of hands grabbed my arm and pulled me out of the torrent of water.

"Thank you, thank you so much. Nate and Manny are right behind me." I smiled at Charlee and the two men helped the others out of the crevasse.

Morley came up out of the lake, "Corbyn, you nudnik, I am ever so pleased to see you."

"As am I to see you alive." I smile at him.

Charlee ran to him and hugged his wet, dripping, icy carcass.

He pushed her away, "Madam please! I am without apparel."

At that moment, a small arm came out of the crevasse. Morley's men grabbed it and pulled out Ta-ta-nee." She opened her eyes and looked at Morley. Without a word, she ran to him and threw herself around him.

He did not complain nor did he push her away. In point of fact, he pulled her in closer and held her for the longest time. She looked into his eyes, "Do dah tee no hay. Mach don tah de!" Her eyes were full of tears.

"She said…" I began.

"I think I got it. She thought I was dead and she was happy to see me alive, right." He smiled at me.

"Close enough. I think she is quite taken by you." I chuckled.

"I hope she feels as strongly about me as I feel about her. She didn't run away after seeing me naked so I guess maybe she does." He smiled at her.

Ta-ta-nee took hold of his face and said, "Hah pay nay, Morley."

Morley's face lit up, "Hah pay nay, Ta-ta-nee." He reached down to kiss her, but she pulled back, "Did I read that wrong? I was going to kiss her."

"I'm sorry Morley; I don't think they know about kissing." I explained.

Charlee walked to me, "We should show her." She put her arms around me and then called Ta-ta-nee, "Ta-ta-nee," She looked back at me, "Hah pay nay, Dub." And she kissed me. I couldn't breathe, but it was fantastic.

Ta-ta-nee watched and then looked at Morley. She put her arms around him and they kissed. I'm pretty sure it was the first time for them both.

Chapter 14

The Unimaginable Wealth In the Eye of the Moon

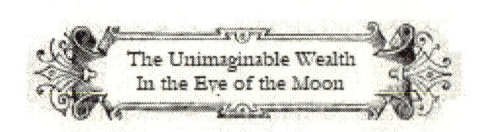

I waited for the smile to fade from Morley's lips, but alas I had to interrupt him while he was still in mid-euphoria, "Morley, if I may, my good man?" I began.

His eyes slowly pulled off the vision in front of him and then he looked at me. The expression on his face was now that of annoyance rather than ecstasy, "What is it Corbyn?"

"Do forgive me, but how is it that you are not dead? We saw you fall off the cliff. For the love of cumquats, how did you do it?" I was excited to hear his tale.

"It actually wasn't a cliff. It was more a hill." His attempt to explain wasn't all I had expected.

"A hill? What on earth do you mean?" I suppose I sounded a bit giddy.

He looked at Ta-ta-nee, "As I fell, I realized the wall was pushing out against me and slowly, I began to scuff along the side like I was on a sledge or a toboggan and before long, I found myself lying at the bottom on my back with most of my clothing torn a bit."

"Plusterpot, I never would have thought it." I looked at Charlee.

He continued, "I sat up and looked about in the darkness. In the far corner, I could see just a hint of morning light, as if morning was just beginning to think of becoming present. I slowly made my way to the brightening light and found myself at the point where we first entered the cavern… you know, where you named it Von Duggery Cavern."

"Goodness me, you were so very lucky." I was still giddy.

"I now understand how they were able to get animals up here, inside the mountain. They brought them up on ropes through the hole in the ceiling." He smiled at Ta-ta-nee.

"How then did you get here just as the avalanche hit, if I may?" I inquired.

He looked away from her and at me, "I couldn't let Ta-ta-nee think that I was dead, so I returned to the Domination and set off to find the lake. The storm was making it difficult, but I wasn't giving up. I saw the lightning hit the side of the mountain and the avalanche start and that's when I saw the lake." He looked back at Ta-ta-nee, "I didn't know what to do. I thought that the rocks would smash through the glass bottom and you would all be trapped."

"You were worried about our safety?" This was unusual to the character of Morley Von Duggery.

He scowled and looked at me, "For some of you, not so much for others, Corbyn."

I laughed aloud, "Touché, my good man. I was worried you were beginning to like me."

"That is not very likely." He half smiled.

I looked at Charlee, "We are here to help. What can we do?"

Morley looked at me. His facial expression changed, "There are three boulders down there that are all rolled against one another. One is worn smooth by the water, I assume it belongs, but the other two could weigh down the quartz and crack it. They have to be removed."

"How do we do that?" Charlee queried.

"My engineer is down there looking now. Perhaps he can come up with something." Morley looked behind him as a man came out of the water.

The gentleman took the tube out of his mouth, "We can't be rollin' thoos out of the pond! It blinkin' well ain't gonna 'appen."

"You're an engineer, figure something out." Morley growled.

I heard someone come up out of the waterfall. I turned around to see Chance and Miss Zadie. Chance took a breath, "I'm an engineer as well, you two, and I think I have a plan. Do you have cargo nets on your ship, Morley?"

"Of course, why?" He looked at Chance questioningly.

"If we wrap one around a stone and then use your airship to drag it along the bottom and out of the water, we should be able to clear the crystal basin enough to make it safe." Chance explained.

"You mean to move one at a time, I presume." Morley looked at his airship.

"Exactly, that would be the best way to go about it, don't you agree?" Chance was a bit giddy as well. Miss Zadie held his arm against her face.

"Yes, I suppose." Morley thought for a moment, "Yes, it just might work."

Morley's engineer rolled his eyes, "Hock, it'll neva wook ah'carse."

"Shut yer gob, Flanagan and get a cargo net." Morley fussed.

Chance and Miss Zadie walked over, "We thought you all should know, the three boulders in a row, down there look just like the monster in the drawings in the cave. Everyone is afraid and worrying that it is going to dig through the quartz." Miss Zadie looked very worried.

Morley brought Ta-ta-nee to us, "Keep her safe for me, will you please?" Then he wrapped in a blanket and ran for his ship.

Charlee looked at me, "He understands that she cannot go with him, doesn't he? She is not part of this world and we can never tell anyone they are here or they risk being destroyed."

"I don't know if he realizes that or not. I do know that he is in love and he does know that." I was unsure of what Morley would do.

A few minutes later, there was a huge winch hanging from the bottom of the Domination. Morley climbed into the operator seat and gave the order to lift off.

Two of his men went into the water with the net and wrapped it around the stone furthest away from shore.

The water had mostly cleared of the mud that had entered earlier, so from underneath the stones were visible as was the rope and the airship with Morley underneath.

Morley pulled the winch tight and the captain began moving the stone toward the opposite shore. Chance looked at the winch, "Morley, it has to go to the downhill side or we risk it rolling back in." He yelled as loud as he could.

Morley nodded and yelled into a tube next to him. The ship slowed and turned about. The rock bumped the other two and then slid slowly to the other shore.

Once it reached the shore, Morley began taking up slack on the line, but instead of the rock coming up, the airship moved down.

Morley yelled into the tube again and the engines of the airship growled like pair of lions. The stone began to lift out of the water and slowly move across the shore line.

"About fifteen feet I should think." Chance yelled.

Morley again nodded and just as the stone had moved to safety he released the winch.

The stone hit the ground and the Domination went up rather quickly. The engines calmed and the ship returned to level.

Nate and Manny ran to the stone to pull the net out, but it was trapped under the boulder, "The rock is sank in the mud and the net won't budge!" Manny yelled at Morley.

"Cut the ropes and get the other net. We haven't time to worry with it." Morley was concerned that the second boulder would be too much on the crystal bottom.

The men did as they were told and the second net was dropped to them. They attached it and Morley sent it to the men in the water.

In a few moments, the second boulder was in the net and headed for the shore. Morley took the slack out of the line and yelled into the tube. The engines growled and the boulder rose from the shore. As the ship moved the boulder swung back and forth. It hit the other stone and then went around it to the downhill side.

Morley released the winch. The boulder hit the other stone and rolled a bit. When it did, the first stone rolled into the net with the second and both began to slide down the mountain, dragging Morley and the Domination down with them.

Ta-ta-nee yelled "Morley!"

I saw that was happening and yelled at Morley, "Cut the rope! Cut the rope!!"

The engines growled an even deeper moan and slowed the stones, but the weight was too great. Morley was trying to cut the rope, but every time he would start, the rope would slip out a bit more.

He looked about for some way to cut the rope when suddenly there was a thud on the side on the basket he was standing in. He looked down and saw Ta-ta-nee pointing to where the sound had been.

Morley looked over the side and saw a hand axe sticking out of the basket. He reached down and grabbed it. Just as he did, the winch reached the end of its rope and the ship jerked. Morley was flung out of the basket and was hanging by the axe and the ship was being pulled down the mountain.

Morley's small thickness made him look like a stick man dangling from a fruit basket. The sight would have been funny had his life and all the lives on the ship not been in jeopardy.

"Heavens, what do we do?" I said aloud for some unknown reason, for I noticed Ta-ta-nee had climbed atop a rock near Morley and jumped.

Her tiny body flew like the thunderbird itself. If she were to miss, she would fall to her doom. Her hands grabbed the side of the basket and she flung herself into the same.

She pulled Morley up and he freed the axe and cut the line. The boulders rolled on down and found a nice ledge to rest side by side on. The captain regained control of the ship and brought her back to us.

As the ship approached, we could see that Morley had Ta-ta-nee in his arms, thanking her properly for saving his life. They both needed a bit of practice at kissing, but I had a feeling they would be working on that between now and the time we left.

Suddenly, we heard an incredible roar coming from underground. The Anasazi were all cheering for Morley. He looked down and saw everyone cheering and waving and he waved back.

Miss Zadie gasped, "It wasn't history that they drew on the wall of the cave; it was a prophecy. Somehow they knew that the mountain would send a monster of sorts and that someone from the sky would save them."

Charlee's eyes grew larger, "You're right. Somehow they knew this day would come." She looked at me, "Then why did Kokopelli send you?"

I smiled, "They didn't send me to give the people hope; they sent me to find their hope. I brought Morley along because I felt it was the right thing to do. I found Morley for them. He was their hope, not any of us."

Charlee kissed me, "You're all the hope I need, Dub."

"You're everything I need, Charlee." I kissed her as well.

I looked at Chance to say something, but he was busy appreciating his wife. I smiled and turned to see the Domination setting down beside the lake.

Morley and Ta-ta-nee walked toward us, hand in hand, "Corbyn, How do you like them apples, I believe is the phrase."

"Bully, my friend, bully. I believe you have saved every one of the Anasazi with the help of the young lady at your side, of course." I smiled.

Morley, looked at Chance and Miss Zadie, "You two are disgusting." He laughed.

Chance turned about, "I believe you two were enjoying one another's company a few moments ago, were you not." He laughed as well.

A young man stuck his head out of the waterfall, "Oon day, oon day. Mah hoo deni."

I looked at everyone, "The elder wants to talk to us all."

Morley looked at Ta-ta-nee and kissed her on the cheek. She smiled and bit her bottom lip then walked to the waterfall and followed the gentleman down.

As we all reached the bottom, the old man walked to Ta-ta-nee, "Da day took nan nay moosk moosk."

Ta-ta-nee looked at Morley and kissed him. They were definitely getting better. She looked back at the old man, "Dah hah nee."

Charlee looked at me, "What was that?"

I laughed, "He asked what they were doing face to face. She told him they were being happy."

"Dah hah nee?" Charlee kissed me and then Miss Zadie kissed Chance.

"Mock tanee shaw dine." The old man blurted out as other couples nearby tried it out.

I laughed, "He thinks it's a sickness that comes over you."

Ta-ta-nee laughed, "Mahanee dah hah nee dinee Dahanee."

"Well, that's interesting. She said, 'Grandfather, try being happy with Grandmother." I explained.

The old man walked to an old woman standing nearby and pressed his lips against hers. He turned around with a smile, "Doday hee nay amah. Das day me hay" He walked back to us.

"What did he say, Dub?" Charlee was quite curious.

"He said it was pleasant and that they should do that tonight." I grinned.

He looked at Morley and then at me, "Sheeshay donee hay tock nay Ta-ta-nee."

I looked at Morley, "He wants to know what you want of Ta-ta-nee"

"What I want of her? I don't understand." Morley was a bit taken aback.

"I think he wants to know your intentions." I offered.

Morley looked at Ta-ta-nee, "I… I … I guess I don't know."

Ta-ta-nee smiled at him, "Hah pay nay, Morley."

Morley smiled, "I want to love her forever."

I looked at the old man, "Hah pay hoos na haho."

The old man smiled, "Nan deehaw noc too dehawn."

I looked at Morley, "He said that it looks like she wants that too."

The old man looked at her, "Shee dah moe hay. Modee hondo nay toc ook."

"He told her she cannot leave. She must stay with her people." I told Morley.

"What?!" Morley's face was quite angry and then it began to smooth out and a look of pain crept onto it, "They cannot risk being discovered. White men would come and destroy everything. I understand that. Why does my chest feel like it is collapsing in on itself?"

"You have a broken heart, Morley." Charlee looked at him. She was so sad for them.

"I… I … can't have a broken… Father has always wanted me to find treasure and when I finally find treasure I can't take her and show her to him." He looked at me, "Corbyn, what am I to do?"

"That is something that is between you and your heart. I can assure you that the young lady will go along with whatever you decide." I smiled.

"You think I should take her and make a run for it?" He asked questioningly.

"Of course not, she would be upset with you for taking her from her people even after her grandfather told you no. I think you need to discuss it with her." I was in earnest.

"How do I talk to her?" He asked and then his face changed to a smile, "Hah pay nay, Ta-ta-nee."

She smiled and took his hand, "Hah pay nay, Morley."

Morley smiled at me, "Corbyn, I now know what you meant." Which was a strange thing for him to say considering I didn't even know what I meant.

Chapter 15

The Unimaginable Wealth In the Eye of the Moon

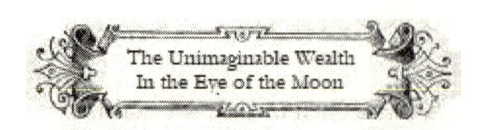

Morley bowed to the old man and took the hand of Ta-ta-nee. They walked away as Morley began trying to communicate with her.

I looked back at the old man, but something behind him caught my eye. There, standing behind all of the other Anasazi, was the figure that I had come to know as Kokopelli. I bowed to the old man and said, "Tone da hah no hay." Which meant something to the effect of, "I'll be right back."

I walked to the figure with many faces. His ever changing faces smiled at me, "Ta mah ho. Dink nah hah tah tok moo noohay." Came into my mind,

"Yes, I finally understood what I was to do." I said aloud.

"Noo hak ten donay, Charlee?" He asked.

"I am very happy with Charlee, why do you ask?" I was a bit confused.

"Po tuck mah ha day chee boy ay." The figure laughed a great and incredibly loud laugh.

I smiled, "Yes, I am sure the old man has many granddaughters, but I love Charlee."

"Tochee dah hanoe chee chin doc hoe." He said.

"I agree with you, she is lovely and very much what I need. I thank you for telling me that Morley would be a friend. He has turned out to be much more even than that." I glanced over at Morley and Ta-ta-nee and then back at Kokopelli.

"Chee, doah hoo nee nay nahee doc han doo nee." He pointed at Morley.

"That is true. We thought he was gone, but he is with us now, as it should be." I smiled.

"Did you really think I would let him die? He is with you now, but will he stay in your company or will he choose the company of another people?" The man of many faces now spoke English, but in many voices.

237

"You can speak English? Yet, you made me speak Anasazi. Why on earth would you change my head for no reason?" I stormed.

"None of this would have been possible if you had not been able to understand and speak to my people. Morley will learn soon. When you leave here, you will not remember how to understand, though your Miss Zadie is picking up on it quite well." He smiled with all his faces.

"Miss Zadie? I suppose she would, she is a linguist after all." I paused, "Wait, is Morley not coming?" I looked back at Morley. When I looked back toward Kokopelli, he started laughing and faded away into the air and the mist from the waterfall.

I turned and looked at Chance and Whitetail. They were looking at me as if a cumquat were growing from my nose. I glanced at Miss Zadie; she was trying to talk to the old man and doing rather well, I might add.

I walked over to Chance, "What was that all about?" Chance still looked confused.

"Kokopelli came to say goodbye." I said.

"You were talking to Kokopelli?" Chance looked like I had lost my mind.

"Yes. You saw me standing there talking to him." I growled.

"We saw you making faced and fussing at the mist coming off the waterfall. Have you lost your senses?" It was obvious they had not seen Kokopelli.

"No, old friend, but perhaps we should think of the predicament of our friend Morley." I looked over my shoulder.

"There is no predicament. He merely has to decide what he already knows he needs to do." Whitetail smiled.

"I suppose you are correct. I am always in awe of those who can change their lives to accommodate the lives of others." I smiled at Whitetail.

"I believe you are about to become one of us, are you not?" Chance laughed.

I had not given it a thought. Chance was right, I was about to change my life to accommodate Charlee, "What am I to do?"

"You are going to go talk to Charlee and find out what you both want from one another and make a rational decision as to how you will live the rest of your life." Chance curled his eyebrow, as he is known to do.

I looked at Charlee, standing beside Miss Zadie. She noticed me and I walked over, "I think we need to talk." Was all I got out.

"Oh, Dub. You know we can't tell anyone of this adventure. These people don't need the help or interference of the outside world." She said.

"I agree, but…" I tried.

Charlee interrupted, "And what of us? You are going back to London. Am I to stay here or am I to move to London or do you have some other plan?"

"Well, I …" I tried again.

"You don't want me tagging around after you do you? I would be an awful bore to you, I'm sure." She was trying to convince herself that she didn't need me or I didn't need her or something.

"Charlee!" I got her attention. She looked into my eyes, "I don't care where we go or what we do as long as you go with me. I don't want you tagging around after me; I want you by my side having adventures together." I took her hands, "You make me happy and I hope I make you feel the same."

Charlee threw her arms around me and kissed me, "I even love the fuzzy beard." She kissed me again.

I looked at Chance and Whitetail. They both had huge smiles on their faces, "My old friend, do you chance the balderdash and falderal?" Chance jested.

"Indeed I will." I looked into Charlee's eyes, pulled the ring my mother gave me off my pinky and got on one knee, "Miss Charlotte, Charlee, will you marry me?"

An angry face came across her face, "Not if you keep calling me Miss Charlotte." A smile crept onto her lips, "Acarse I'll marry ya, Dub, I love you."

I slid the ring on Charlee's finger, "As I love you." I looked at Morley. He was on his knee as well, "How is Morley talking to Ta-ta-nee?"

"Love knows no language, Dub. He loves her and she loves him, that's all the language they need, us as well." She pulled me up to kiss her.

Chance, Whitetail and Miss Zadie cheered. The old man put his hand on my shoulder, "Chee moho tin nay."

I looked at Charlee, "He said we are united which I assume means married to these people."

The old man walked toward Morley and Ta-ta-nee. He put his hand on Morley's shoulder and I assume said the same thing.

Morley took Ta-ta-nee's hand and ran back to us, "We are married!" He said.

"Congratulations, Morley. Charlee and I are married as well." I smiled.

"Sorry Dub, we will need to make it legal, but I believe Morley and Ta-ta-nee won't need any other legalities." She smiled at Morley.

"Thank you Charlee. Yes, it is true. I am staying with Ta-ta-nee. I can learn their ways and I can teach them a few things as well." He smiled at me, "Thank you Corbyn."

"For what? What have I done?" I fussed.

"You believed in me. You believed in the fact that somewhere, deep inside, there was good. I know I have never made it easy, but I have always wanted a friend. I hope we are, if nothing else, friends." He stuck out his hand.

"Friends we are and friends we shall stay wherever we go. No matter where I go, I shall always have a soft spot for the man who shot me with a cannon." I laughed and took his hand.

"You may take the Domination. Would you please seek out my father and tell him that I finally found the world's greatest treasure and I intend to spend the rest of my life with her." He pulled Ta-ta-nee close.

"You know that your coming was foretold, don't you?" I looked at him.

"Foretold? What do you mean?" He looked at me as Chance and Whitetail were looking at me earlier.

"The drawings in the cave were predictions. You were the sun god who killed the rock monster and then waved at the people below." I smiled.

"I am no hero." He said.

"Oh, but you are a hero. You have saved the lives of so many of us. You like to pretend that your friends mean nothing to you, but you are a softy at heart. I think this young lady is a very, lucky lady." I shook his hand.

"Corbyn, you're not a bad person at all. I am sorry I shot you with a cannon." I knew that was as close to an apology as I was going to get.

I turned and looked at Charlee, "Am I staying in America with you or are you coming with me?"

"I'm coming with you if you promise there will be much more adventure." She came to me.

"Indeed there will be, my love, adventures extraordinaire!" I put my arm around her and leaned her back and kissed her.

Whitetail walked over, leaned down and whispered in my ear, "You can drop me in Salida, Boss."

I started laughing, "We would be honored to do so, my friend."

The old man took Ta-ta-nee's hand and put his other hand on Morley's back, "Maha nee do nay sayhooday." He laughed.

I started laughing. Charlee shook my arm, "What did he say?"

"He said he would teach Morley to be a good husband." I was still laughing.

Morley didn't find it as funny, but he knew he had a lot to learn to live among the Anasazi, "Shee … doon…. Mohay… I think."

"You said that you would try. I assume that is correct." I grinned at Ta-ta-nee.

Ta-ta-nee smiled and laid her head on Morley's shoulder and whispered, "Maha nee do nay sayhooday, sheeshay."

I whispered in Charlee's ear, "She said she would teach Morley to be a good husband herself."

"Corbyn," Morley began, "You should come and check on us again soon. I will miss my friends."

"Indeed we shall, my good friend." I shook his hand again and hugged Ta-ta-nee. We all exchanged pleasantries and climbed up to the Domination.

Once we were all on board, we met on deck to watch the take off. Charlee took my arm and wrapped herself around it, "When are we getting married?" She asked.

"That would be up to you; the sooner the better to my way of thinking." I kissed her forehead.

"The captain said he would love to marry us, if you are willing." She looked up at me.

"Perfect. That will give is something to do on our way to South America." I smiled.

"South America?" Charlee was confused, "A honeymoon?"

The airship was now high in the air, "If you like, but I think we have a pirate treasure to find, 5° 8 minutes 3 seconds north, 58° 59 minutes 0 seconds west." I smiled and held her tight, "Adventurers Extraordinaire, I like it."

The Unfathomable Series of Adventures will continue, but for now….

THE END

5° 8 minutes 3 seconds North, 58° 59 minutes 0 seconds West

∞

Made in the USA
Middletown, DE
27 June 2021